Time

for

the

Dead

a "Zombies - A Love Story" novella by
Mike Gutowski

The struggle is real for Witches, Zombies and Humans
in the hundo p crazy West Kansas plains.

Mike Gutowski

Time for the Dead is a work of fiction. Names, characters, places and incidents are the products of the author's imagination or are used fictitiously. Any resemblance to actual events, locales or persons, living or dead, is entirely coincidental.

Cover artwork by Alan Tham of Alan Tham's Art.

For permission requests, contact the publisher, at:
Email: dadx3g@msn.com
Twitter: @dadx3gMike
Facebook: @mike.gutowski.62
Instagram: www.instagram.com/mike.gutowski.62/
Word Press: cratchandothernovelsbymikegutowski.com

Printed in the United States of America

ISBN: 978-1-7333895-0-1
eBook ISBN: 978-1-7333895-1-8

1. Horror. 2. Science Fiction. 3. Dark Fantasy.

First Edition

There are two ways of spreading light: to be the candle or the mirror that reflects it.

---Edith Wharton

Then the seventh angel blew his trumpet, and there were loud voices in heaven, saying, "The kingdom of the world has become the kingdom of our Lord and of his Christ, and he shall reign forever and ever." And the twenty-four elders who sit on their thrones before God fell on their faces and worshiped God, saying, "We give thanks to you, Lord God Almighty, who is and who was, for you have taken your great power and begun to reign. The nations raged, but your wrath came, and the time for the dead to be judged, and for rewarding your servants, the prophets and saints, and those who fear your name, both small and great, and for destroying the destroyers of the earth."

---Revelation 11:15-18

Blessed are the meek: for they shall inherit the earth.

---King James Version, Matthew 5:5

Also, by Mike Gutowski:
CRATCH
available on Amazon.com as soft cover book or e-book.

Mike Gutowski

To my daughters,
who provide invaluable life perspective
I appreciate every day.

Contents

Prologue

Zombies: A Love Story
6

Part One

Trumpets
8

Part Two

Regenerations
78

Part Three

Revelations
101

Prologue

Zombies: A Love Story

It had become okay to play with dead things. Just had to be careful. Dead things may bite. In the places where farmers ruled as King or Queen, and cattle meandered as prey, a West Kansas town's fresh aroma of butchered beef surfed an invisible wind. A tart cow pooh scent pinched up the nostrils of tourists and short time visitors, but the locals were immune to the aroma. Wheat fields more than danced a jig amidst the wind's soft music. The wind carried a poison, unknown to a local farmer who had purchased, on the cheap, some bags of grain rejected by a sleazy out of town producer trying to make a fast buck on experimental seed product. Such was the risk and mystery of the farming ritual from year to year, sometimes from season to season. The town of Meadow City was a place where the hunger for food, for profit, for provenance the devil had noticed, so accordingly the un-sainted one dangled ethereal fables of quick riches amid the border towns. The tainted grain was sowed into the soil carpet, then nurtured in the ground for a few seasons, only to fail in quality and breadth upon the appropriate harvest time, when the product of the seed served useless except for a mysterious platitude of misery.

An open, barren plain just outside Meadow City, located about thirty or so miles east of the Colorado border, spotted by short, green grass mixed into higher beige patches, beckoned the lonely in spirit. There was one exception to this serene scene.

One spot was dotted mostly by old gravestones sticking out of the ground and tucked under a lone, high cottonwood tree, where no seed wanted to grow. The tree stood as a monument to the Lincoln family who had settled this spot of ground generations ago, alone. Behind the tree a walking path led up to and over a hill.

Wind almost always blew in and around, sometimes funneled from the sky above, as a trance amidst the West Kansas plain and folk and nature's wonders. There was no escape. It had become kin to all that lived and breathed. If the wind ever had stopped, the absence acted as a bad omen. The meaning of no wind sprung silently among the townspeople the imminent horror of a tornado come to life.

On this day, the wind remained the wind, caressed the leaves of the cottonwood. All was at peace and on pace for serenity of the usual West Kansas moments of fealty to the land and to the life bestowed in a wealth of familial blessings abundant in such a place. The story unfolded like napkin linen skillfully placed upon the lap of an eatery patron who harbored a voracious appetite.

Mike Gutowski

PART ONE

Trumpets

Chapter One

The wind could be a little mean sometimes; more so than humans. He knew how mean in nature people could act, although in this place, people he hadn't seen in quite a while. "Only the lonely knew how much such a situation truly stung," he thought. He saw not a thing in a longer while. Best dreams sometimes materialized to him as nightmares. He knew such, yet still subjected himself; surrendered his thoughts to the dream interlude. "No choice," he thought. Better to dream than become trapped in the darkness. He had been trapped in it for a long time. The search for escape, although weary, gave him something to do. The darkness unforgiving, stuck him in all the highest pain places of his body but particularly in the middle of his back; prodded, until demons interceded. Darkness demons of all shapes, sizes, odd forms terrorized his sleep time, yet he didn't try to ignore them, the dreams or the demons.

Sometimes the dark place and the ephemeral mysterious beings provided the only solace in a long night, or what he perceived to be night, as there was no light around him from below, above or anywhere near him. He was forced to imagine light to escape the darkness. He didn't know why he was sent to this place. Resigned himself, he had, to the inevitability of darkness and what may come from it. Such thoughts leapt towards his psyche as fleas hopped into and surfed upon a summer air. "No choice," he thought once more.

The wanderings of his mind startled him into another consciousness, or at least what he perceived as such a state. The darkness acted like a screen upon which his thoughts, sometimes in words and sometimes in images appeared. He had a three-fix rule. If the object or person didn't stay repaired after three tries, there was a reason, so he left each alone. Darkness. Cats don't smile. He guessed they didn't need to. Humans, on the other hand, had the need. Darkness. He wondered where squirrels retreated to when they were dying. Did they hide to die in peace at the old rodent's home? This dark place oiled his thoughts.

Perhaps, to comfort himself in the place of long and wide and smothering darkness, his still sentient mind concocted a mnemonic name for the blackness of alone time: Gadasol. This cognitive invention, calmly extracted after long intellectual reflection, sprung from the words "Goodness and dark along steps of light." He didn't know what or why or how these thoughts came to him. Maybe there were fairies lurking in the darkness. As a human, he learned long ago that the pretty things were often revealed as the most dangerous representations, masks, for the most awful realities. So, he suffered the dreams to understand them. After all, it was impossible to suffer only the light forever. He tried to defeat the dark. He imagined it as a soft, warm blanket of sheep's wool. An elegant tone sounded in his head. He recognized the sound. His above ground days acclimated him to musical enjoyment; a taste he could relish all his own, unbridled from the sensibilities of society; as he had resided so far from it, at the dawn of some lonely times. When the loneliness resided in his mind, uncomfortably, from dawn to dusk, he surrendered to it. For now, and for then. On tick and on tock. In sound and fury. By charge or by chance. Comfort callously eluded the better angels of his nature. His best efforts no longer guided him. Stripped bare, he was, of any semblance to sense or sensibility. A familiar tune interrupted his unimpeded and rapid fall into a darkness darker than the darkest dark he could imagine.

The smooth as satin voice of Johnny Ace purred words of "The Clock" into his mind; offered some comfort to his discontented soul. An unquivering discomfort posed by the unknown act-induced imprisonment steadily faded. "Is this experience just another part of my life?" He wondered about the debacle. "Just like the kitchen plumbing," he surmised. Stopped working. He raged against the will of the clog, but the demon mixes of hair, food particles, and mystery substances fought back so dogged in determination a stubborn mule would finish first in the race. The fight provided him only muscle discomfort in his arms, shoulders, neck and near-busted temporal lobes. He pushed and pulled the plunger so many times he lost count. Gurgles and bubbles and belches booted and rebooted in sounds of great distress. A cruel foe, this demon. Suddenly, the sink drained again, yet only at almost half speed. Perhaps the plumbing stubbornness was a sign; of what, he was uncertain; but after three separate tries over a month's worth of weeks, he bowed to the will of the plumbing pipe gods as other chores and their intricate as spider-web matters begged like hungry new-born chicks for his "feed me" attention and special skills. Only enough time for half-done plagued his days and allowed multiple distractions to pile up like cinder blocks on his mind.

Above his head appeared a speck of light. He thought it was light, but in this place, certainty twirled a ring around him as steadily as Polka dancers. The light speck gave not clues. He sniffed the air to interpret the threats that may hide in the dark cloak of his confinement. No clues exposed themselves. His sense of smell was inexplicably stunted. Fear arose inside of him as smell was usually a barometer for any degree of trouble he might encounter in the surroundings, but scent was at this moment no longer an active ally. Such betrayal heightened his fear of the darkness even further. A quick change in thought might capture and mask such fear, he considered. He attempted an imagined walk along the path of a new thought to escape. He began to find his mind drowning in the river flow of the fear. His arms would not move at his mental commands. His legs would not kick, even in his crowded imagination.

He tried to author a book once. He recounted his notes. They floated into his darkness television screen. When he looked up at the stars which he knew must be there despite his blindness; the wonder of what it all meant pierced his heart like a steely sword. Was there anyone out there; have they ever been here; are they benevolent or as devious and dangerous as humans? He also looked inward, at the moral compass; wondered why humans treated each other so badly. Reading a person's mind seemed to become a farmer's skill; or at least interpreting the eye movements and subtle twists of the head at the neck. A combination of the two themes crisscrossed his literary works and too, his lost real world. Another dimension, maybe, he had accidentally stepped into while working the fields of his farm.

He developed a routine to rid himself of the black, blank screen, but it was fraught with horrid visions before he could erase the board completely and start onto a new thought. He flew to the moon to see better the stars, Jupiter and Mars, then fell from a cliff in a storm of rain and hail as fists of darkness punched at his jaw. He could take a punch and he knew it, so he didn't jiggle his imagination just yet, to appreciate and stand down the full effect of each energy burst. The horrors still attacked him, turning multiple white cloud puffs into dark, long strips of a whip. He surrendered to the storm's force. He thought it might bring some new insight. He tried to form a smile in his face to mask a broken heart sense of it all. Whether he could beam a smile remained uncertain. Physical feeling evaded him like the fox on a moonlit night as visions appeared in disconnected puzzle pieces.

First, a large eye came into view. The eye was staid, unblinking; unadorned by any hint of thread-like lashes; naked of them. The unblinking eye covered the whole screen. He stared at it; tried to stare it down; will it away. It reacted by morphing at the pupil area until the pupil became snake or demon like in shape, turned oval and vertical. Eventually, the eye dissolved from his view, then blew away in the same manner as wind-blown desert sand. The screen became empty except for the black. Then, odd green shapes of no geometric form appeared; random shapes like ink blots. He waited as he knew they would degenerate. These visions randomly played and plagued his mind even when he wasn't in this dark place. Once the visions had disappeared and all was black again, the faces would come into view.

The faces were deformed, like sock puppets yet to be completed; some devoid of a button eye, or yarn hair strands, or magic marker lips. After the sock puppets' visions, his mind was invaded by human-like face forms, but only distorted, squashed or mashed up faces. Eyes popped where the ears should be; noses where the chin would protrude; some hairless, some mostly hairy; none shaped like the familiar oval of the true human form, at least the form he grew up to perceive and know in the West Kansas countryside. A certain relief faintly overcame his random thoughts upon the memory blotch click of his point of earth origin. Since the faces were so misshaped, his mind tried to fill in the blank spots; to squish and roll and punch at them like soft clay putty. He could only do such with his mind. It took a while until human faces finally appeared as pasted onto the shape of mortal heads. He could only see the heads, not even a hint of the neck. The heads floated in and out of his view; sometimes bobbed as if in water; sometimes sunk low and only in the corners of his vision; other times erased by an unseen hand as soon as they materialized. He could make no sense of it. He determined after much of this nonsense activity a plan. Go with it. See where it ends up. Get rid of it at all costs if discomfort interceded, yet the temptation to see on into the end of the story was great. He usually regretted the effort. Still, the mystery of it all soothed him enough to relax his mind for a bit.

He briefly wondered if all humans encountered such visions in the dark, or in dreams, or once the eyes were closed. The odd nature of the visions displayed began to spur in him a strong belief, or churned a desperately clawed at hope, that he was still alive, somewhere; but the origin of his presence in this darkness still hid from his perception like a stealth rat under the shed. He remembered the rat remained invisible for quite a while. Only sounds of scratches or the rustle of small objects like abandoned crooked nails or threaded screws betrayed a presence. Perhaps the probing rat was chased away or killed and eaten by a dog; or hunted and swooped upon and grasped tightly in the sharp, curved talons of a hungry hawk, then sped away, upward into the sky. "Goodbye, rat. See your kin soon," he teased. He had yet to reach the destination in the blackness where his predicament would be explained. Still he feared a rat's fate could somehow swoop down upon him and grasp and rip at whatever or whoever he existed as now. Salvation hope remained steady amidst his knowledge to not trust people; a learned skill of significant benefit. Still, he could not recall the trigger for such a bullseye conclusion.

He tried to remember his name, but the iron silence rang loud in his head. Bells of interminable stillness clanged louder and louder until he could no longer see the vision path except through a cloudy, cataract blotted pane of glass, but not actual glass, only imagined. He cursed, though his lips wouldn't move. Now he would have to start all over, from the lonely beginning, through the maze of ugly scenes, unable to avoid any of them, into the mousetrap of uncertain fate. He wondered if he had somehow stumbled into another dimension. The local library housed books about fantasy worlds of alternate universes. Maybe that was the location of his prison now; an alternative place where he had not yet gained enough knowledge to navigate.

He remembered the story of the cubes by a little-known deceased Slavic author, dismissed by his peers, unpopular in his life, but discovered as an innovator of the written word and fantasy worlds, after his death. The author's fate caused him concern, but he knew it was difficult to escape such a cage. Only a brazen lust for popularity was lost. Someone, readers, other authors benefitted from the experimentation of the author. Perhaps that was enough even after death to claim a modest level of success; a horizontal plane only the author could appreciate in full. Such was the risk of all attempts at betterment, as he knew well toiling on the farmland. He was a farmer. The memory trips worked despite their bizarre nature. Life glorious reigned during success, as long or short as it lasted. Famine and shame tolled for them in failure.

His family, at least he assumed a family existed, as his recall was quite challenged in his present state, were well acquainted in the latter experience. Family. He tried to remember them. He couldn't exactly. A son, a daughter, he recalled connections to such but started to believe part of his damnation involved lack of enough memory, somehow smothered by the darkness; to prevent him from making more sentient connections; to figure it all out. Still, the ignition of thought about a family encouraged him, in West Kansas, amidst fields, perhaps to toil the land as a farmer. He must have had one or all of these life experiences if they entered his mind now.

He had time, he considered, to remember and explore all aspects of the familial relationships, then more accurately determine the measure of his successes or failures engendered by such activity. The thought comforted him to a certain degree. In his head, a musical tune sounded. "What is This Thing Called Love," he recognized as the tune by artist Cole Porter, the 1929 version, his favorite, or perhaps it was now his favorite. It played over and over. There were still some days when the birds seemed to like whatever the wind brought forth; at least his memories told him so. Memories. A pound of flesh for each he had given, in life and in this dark place. A new torture had been foisted upon his soul, he thought, a new torture.

His mind wandered to the next random thought. Gods, demons and spirits were part of every culture. These entities played a part in many life stories. He had acquired some books on these subjects, more reading than he could accomplish given the truncated pleasure time of a farmer's world, but every time he completed some literary mastication time, his thought processes were stimulated into overdrive. He regretted his inability to fully comprehend the subject matter nuances of some studies such as certain aspects of physics, astronomy, biology. He learned of the plasma-based universe; humans carbon based. Humans were thus stuck on the earth dirt; couldn't interact in other dimensions despite a learned ability to free themselves from the dirt. He wanted to learn more, remember more, contemplate more except the darkness had snared him. His darkness pastime involved therapeutic thoughts of flipping up both middle fingers to an imagined television screen while it colorfully beamed a comical display of multitudinous, mealy-mouthed media mushers.

For no apparent reason he could discern, he remembered a taste of a soup he liked much. He reflected upon the soup including appearance and smell. A local restaurant, although the vicinity of the locality he couldn't pinpoint, but the taste, aroma, steaminess of it tweaked a pleasant memory of the smell into his head. Remember the name he couldn't. A good and valuable mind occupier it was to try and recall the name of the soup and the ingredients, as well. Soup, soup, broth in a shiny brown mug around which his hands could reach and melt into the warmth of it. Soup, the name, the appearance of the contents evaded his effort. Since he considered the effort worthwhile, his mind persisted upon the mountain climb to reach the peak of an exquisite recollection. He could smell it well; view the contents bob and soak as if alive. The name elusive remained, yet the challenge stimulated him further. Two words were involved in the name. The first word seemed not appropriate for soup, but he remembered it as pasta. The next word gave him fits to remember. Gol? Gil? He waited patiently while his mind inhaled the soup aroma. A song infected him. He tried to rid himself of it and return to the soup imagination, then a warm tap inside him emerged, from the song thought of "Do, re, mi, fa, so ...". Fa. Fa was the sound. The soup that made sounds in him was how he used to remember it. Fagioli. Pasta Fagioli. Of course. Just the words agitated a taste of pleasure along his tongue. Tomato sauce broth hugged together a mix of varied ingredients such as bits of sausage, varied beans and further accompanied by bits of tomato, onion and garlic. His imagination greedily tasted into the top layer of soup. Each dip of the spoon unto the soup marked a magnificence of moment. Moment one, moment two, moment three and more he re-imagined until he was full.

The soup smell lingered upon his lips. Then he debated whether the search for the memory of the soup name, or the memory of the broth aroma, or the memory of the ingredients involved greater pleasure than the memory of the taste of the combined ingredients at a rate of one spoonful at a time. He had lost his way in the soup. His mind had filled of the soup thoughts until they busted over the edge of the bowl and fell in a waterfall's dash upon his darkness. The darkness. It was the place his mind always returned. He waited for the next moment to reveal itself, however random and sneaky it might approach. He determined to not become further afraid. He imagined a Saint-Saens cello concerto, "The Swan", as a course for relaxation. Sleeping. "I must be sleeping." He couldn't find an escape hatch for the sleep thought.

He travailed upon the long lonely path further as the concerto slowly faded out. Whether he was alive, dead, or somewhere in the between became no longer certain to him. The in between contemplation caused him much concern. He had no perspective to set it in place. His life experiences always had him somewhere doing and breathing the inhales and exhales shackled to his body. He tried to move his head. The movements, only slight, created crackle sounds of saltines. He was glad his head could move but the resulting sounds disturbed him. Perhaps to follow the light would help as there was nothing else to do, but the constraints of his confinement were not visible. The dim speck of light still betrayed his better efforts to understand. He commanded a movement from his arms, yet they failed to hear his thoughts.

A voice invaded his head. He listened as best he could in the darkness. It was a woman's voice. An energy began to grasp his body. The voice of Nat King Cole crooned "The Very Thought of You", soothed him. Repeatedly he analyzed the sound, the tonal inflections. He tried to attach a face to the voice through an intense gaze into his mind to find an image of the lips and the skin tone and tenderness around the lips. The voice became a spark. The spark sounded a fizz in his head, yet not a light. The energy, punched into his gut by the sound, flexed forth and back. Try as he might, a complete face would not reveal itself to him. He knew the voice as harbinger of something good to come; or it had sprung from one of his memories like a sprite in the woods; random and pleasant and fresh as the smooth curved shine of an unbitten apple. He remembered one of his favorite songs, while in the woman's presence, and especially when she was not and he suffered only his vision of her; the elixir effect of her smell aroma; the glow her smooth light skin emanated; the spray of her blonde, long hair which sparkled a tint, almost like a halo from the top of her head. Cole's "Stardust" melody interceded; laid his mind to rest for a bit.

So, it went on for him like this, over and over; dark emptiness pitted by seeds of intellectual light bursting like flipped Joker cards from the deck of his burning, silent emptiness. There was no end to it. On and on, a clay pigeon of inspirational thought, or of sappy memory, projected into the sky, which he could not see except from his mind, then a loud crack, snap, and all in the air was shattered pottery solemnly descending towards and then onto the ground. Bright lights of hope would beam out of his mind like Cole's "Fascination", then cracked like firecrackers, then burrowed into silence.

Thoughts of callous words and derision speared his mind. The sounds he traced to the lips on the face of the woman. Another spark of energy gripped his body, the muscles tensed. Now the darkness pressed against his chest, his abdomen, his waist and all below it. Now it hammered upon his brow. His entire body felt heavy, as if it had transformed into a boulder. The boulder tried to break through the hard object upon which it was compressed. Harder and stiffer, flatter as a strange feeling of multiple hands rooted up from the darkness below him as weeds. The weeds engulfed his being, then attempted to retract, tugged him along.

He now much wished his mind would shut down to give him rest from the horrible uncertainty of his plight. "My way," he thought. Where was he and why was his body feeling these strange feelings and his mind wandering like a wounded deer after the buckshot sound of uncertain destination? He wasn't really feeling any physical pain, only some discomfort, but the mental anguish ebbed and flowed into unrelenting status. A guilty feeling sucker punched him on the chin. Did he make other people feel the way he was now feeling? A taste of his own medicine was more bitter than he realized it could have been. Apologies unheard now stung the inside of the mouth like bitter herbs, but again, he didn't feel it in his mouth. He felt it only in his mind. The imaginations of pain were pain itself to the body part connected to the thought.

He searched for a way to shut off his thoughts. If he could escape this darkness, he could drink it away. He remembered his number one drinking rule: never bring alcohol into the field. The thought of the moving thresher rolling over him and slicing him into pieces to be splayed upon the land freaked him out mightily. He usually entered a prayer state as soon as possible once the thought exploded into his brain so it could put up a defensive wall until the limb shudders escaped.

The thought of his first love burned into his mind. The passion of it pinched him like static electricity. The inevitable cliff falls into jagged rocks below followed once the crush had crashed. The visor-like pressure of the emptiness after, chased him wherever he went; rampaged after his thoughts and ravaged away at any semblance of love capture. His mind had become the fox target of hunting hounds.

Then the thought he had long ago pushed to the back of his mind stabbed him in the back. Perhaps he was dead, and his current situation was the status of the dead; to be somewhere that was nowhere yet conscious of the fix. Tortured by this thought, a migraine headache began a slow boil in his brain. He wanted to rub the side of his head, but he could not elicit a response from his shoulder or bicep or elbow or forearm. He failed to ascertain whether his hand still existed in a form that could accomplish a rub. A positive thought emerged from the migraine. "I can feel it." Then he wondered if the pain reflected his active imagination. Still, if he could imagine, that meant something. His mind still worked. He reasoned it would not still work, or he would not have an awareness of it working, if he was dead. He had never been dead, as far as he could recall, so another yellow dead-end signpost presented itself. He remembered, during his reading, a brain could still function for up to about eight minutes after death. Had eight minutes passed?

If his brain still functioned, then his senses may still operate. His mind raced down the checklist. He heard nothing. He felt nothing except the migraine pain and that moment could have been a memory. He saw nothing except what he thought was a tiny light above him. The migraines sometimes showed sparks to him, so he remained unsure.

He must be alive, he thought, or how else could he be thinking? "I am; therefore, I think." He intentionally reversed Descartes theory, as had Nietzsche, in search of a spark to alight the tinder of his thoughts. He tried to say it. Repeatedly he tried to say it, but his mouth could not form the words, or at least, he could not feel his mouth move. Still, he felt a migraine. That meant something. In this dark place, he could still feel something. When he was in the light, his questions comforted him; told him he was still alive; proved to him his freedom regardless of the constraints posed by his birth life, childhood, and personal interactions and decisions. Now, he could do nothing physically, or he could not feel doing anything physical. His thoughts in this place started to appear like the bars of a jail. He knew the process of the jailhouse system. He had earned his time on an emotional punch moment; or a temper tantrum in a moment of public rage against someone he deemed dangerous, or stupid, or woke. "I'd rather be awake than woke," he imagined as a thought. Woke seemed, to him, a dead state of petulant conformance. To be awake and woke was the worst curse possible to impose on the mind of another human being. It was for this reason he believed many higher institutions of learning were no different than Satan worshippers. To be woke was to be awake but not intelligent. To be woke was to allow others to put you in a box upon which escape was impossible. To him, the box became a cradle for the mentally unintelligible. The woke were afraid of their own spider. "Okay," he scolded. Negativity doesn't allow an escape means. "Had to try it anyway." There must be at least a worm's squirm of chance to awake in a better fitted place. His thoughts flicked like fly wings, then stopped as the fly legs batted like human lashes.

He imagined a spider and conversed with it viscerally. The spider crept up closer to him; along his stomach; then upon his chest; eventually onto his chin; finally, at the bridge of his nose. The spider's eyes glowed like diamond sparkle. The tiny, lonely speck of light above engaged the spider's eyes in a magical fashion. "Thank you for being here with me, Mr. Spider." The spider stared. "You are looking good, Mr. Spider." The spider stared. "How's the family." He didn't really want to know the answer to this question because he knew a spider's family of young could number in the hundreds. The spider stared. A distant low voice said, "Adam." He surmised the spider wasn't much of a talker, so the voice origin mystified him. Then a realization came. He could see his face in the spider's eyes as the pinhole light from above shined a glow onto them. He saw many of his own faces. He didn't look too good. His face reflection seemed ashen and gray at the spot where the spider's eye-glow ricocheted back. The realization was briefer than brief because the spider moved along the bridge of his nose, across his forehead, and out of his line of imagination sight. He could not feel the spider's leg touches upon his head. He could not hear the spider trenching around in his hair.

This journey, he sensed, ineffectual as presented, wasn't the first upon which no path would open; when no light guided; where no purpose shone; how no destination hung like a Christmas ornament on the far edge of the horizon. He refused to take responsibility for the predicament, yet, such a thought path offered no solutions; only forsaken and moldy conclusions jumped forth into the rising weeds of contemplation. The cursed and cloudy mist of "why" hovered above, then dropped heavy upon him in a traitor's alliance formed in the company of the darkness. Such a foe he had never faced.

An escape he needed from his imagination, yet, his only means left of escape remained imagination; and the ultimate destination always led to a dead end of more imagination. He scrolled through a list of his favorite music tunes, but the tones rushed at him so fast he could not decide on a tune except melancholy notes of woe. Darkness plus woe could only result in defeat. He refused to allow his desperate situation a victory. "I must be alive," he deduced, else how could Descartes's reasoning emerge. Perhaps Nietzsche was correct. Thinking didn't exist in the "I" unless there existed a "we" into which the thought could be consumed. Even the sense of "I" could be a conglomeration of thoughts inimical to the thinker. He started to believe he remained alive, in what form uncertain to him, yet, alive still.

Alive dead. Dead alive. He rested his thoughts upon the softest pillow he could imagine. He didn't want to fall into another hole of darkness. He feared there might be multiple levels of darkness and his mind could send him to worse and worse levels. Perhaps Dante's Inferno was a darkness that only became darker and still darker until the dark layers became so heavy, no escape remained. For a second, he thought he shuddered, or rather, his body shuddered; or perhaps he imagined the shudder. "I must stop thinking." And in the thought, he sunk another layer low. He had become a Lord of the flies in the east of Eden. Too morbid, even for a West Kansas farmer burdened by a hopeless quest against insurmountable odds, he had become. Wait. Why did that thought become born? He didn't know whether to abort it or suckle it closer to his breast and protect and help it to grow, slowly, strong, and stronger. Dead alive. Alive dead.

He failed at almost every effort of calm. Another thought spark lit into him. An autopsy would have been ordered if he died, maybe. If his body was so obviously destroyed beyond the hope of life, then maybe no. The woman's face looked out upon him, but he could not see a body attached. He tried a longer view, but this wish wasn't accommodated. Of two things he was sure: he still had a body; his mind still functioned. Strangely, he could not detect any movement in his chest. Surely, if he was still breathing, his chest would announce the activity. He tried to blow air through his nose. Nothing happened. He tried to inhale through his mouth. Nothing happened. As it suddenly struck to him, he might be buried underground, a panic pinched hard into his side, like a runner's stitch. The bad news: no escape. The good news: he felt the stitch, or at least imagined it. As a cognitive capability, use of imagination gave him some hope. His brain remained alive, for thought, but apparently, for nothing else. "I must be dead," he concluded. "I hope they didn't autopsy me." The horrid thought provoked his energy level. He had seen an autopsy performed, once, when one of his neighbors, years ago, died in a tornado storm. The medical examiner allowed him to assist as so many of the examiners were out in the field, recovering the dead.

Autopsy. The word was a twisted, barbed wire coiled sentence, to his mind. The unraveling of a person's body; remove the parts, the organs; weigh, measure; the weight device metal clinked and ticked; the measure device scratchily rubbed while extended; the putting back together in a tidy, neat, patted manner like a UPS packing box machination. Didn't make him ill. He was glad of that. A farmer to become ill around the hauntings of injury, maiming and death would have been unnatural, particularly given the sounds and smells of the meat packing plant down the road, a bit of a ways from the local farms. He sensed he was still intact, reason unknown. If he was in fact dead and buried, he hoped his kin abided by his wish to skip embalming. He was no

Pharaoh, no King, no Royal creature in need of post death immortality. He preferred to let nature merge with him in the body and mind, untainted by oils, fluids; devoid of pretty sewing and gooey gluing and cleaning of this and that and in-between and inside. He wanted to be potted underground as is, except for a pine box containment. His thought was the box may be needed for any travels post-death he may have not become accustomed or acclimated to due to incorrect thinking on his part. He wouldn't have to stand all day on clouds, waiting in line; or bake on the stove if he ended up on the wrong side of the heavenly ledger. At least, he could use the wood for something.

He had heard, from a source during a drunk stage of time, hell could be a nasty cold place, if it wasn't a boiling cauldron or burning cavern. Of course, he couldn't escape the notion that no place was better than these destinations. He rested fine in that thought. A place free from worry, even if not in a sentient state, preferably not, would do. All of those days he never wanted to reveal thoughts through his facial muscles, but what he really thought now squeezed at him.

He tried to sleep, or at least to relax. He wondered if he gave his brain a rest, then he could regenerate inside his body and perhaps break free, physically, from the confines of this darkness that haunted him like a plague. A blackness death. At least he was fairly certain he lay on his back. If so, then he was facing the stars. If only he could learn to bridge the gap between his back and the stars, then maybe space would open for him to escape. Maybe some rest would give his limbs the power he needed to find, to create an opening in one of the walls of dark matter surrounding him. He was almost sure he witnessed, at a minimum, a pinhole of light above, although his awareness of it no longer prevailed in his mind. The migraines could be cruel and deceitful in that way.

It was the time for the woman's face to come back into his mind. He stared at it for a long time. He could not see her physical details, except those of the face. He felt compelled to make a stand on this search for meaning in the woman's face. His earlier attempts had failed to define her identity and how such knowledge could help define him.

Of the memories he recaptured, none were of recent origin, at least, recent enough for him to understand how he ended up in this dark place. Something was happening above him. He was almost certain. It wasn't something from his imagination. It wasn't. It couldn't be; or it never was and here he would remain imprisoned for the rest of his time. He had no idea what this thought meant, the rest of his time. What time? What for? Yet, he knew something was about to happen. He was even more resolved in the thought he would act, as ready and violent as needed to free himself and once again reign as the master of the place just above his body. Only such manner of thinking could allow hope an access to overcome the stale and sour status of his present condition.

The black screen started to activate again like a shaken Magic eight ball, just as he contemplated a surrender accompanied by truce offers to the darkness. So many thoughts espoused; so little time to figure them. A blurred word floated and swayed, then came into focus. Adam. The word was Adam. It meant something; maybe it had meaning for him. The name faded, disappeared, and the blackness rained down like hale, then swayed in mysterious wind, then rose like a North Sea storm of epic proportion. Something was happening --- to Adam --- to him. Who could it be, this Adam?

Chapter Two

At the front of one smooth, shiny gravestone, several dozen of which pock-marked the landscape, close in front of the lone cottonwood tree, a human head poked out of the ground in tandem to the rising of the morning sun, announced in concert by an eardrum split of a rooster's chime, trumpeted loud, and clear, and shrill as the wind's bitter slap of an invisible hand. Above the head, the gravestone revealed a thinly chiseled hint of a word and numbers: May 5, 1955. The head munched on a black squirrel. The squirrel families in this part of West Kansas had developed extended patches of furry skin as an evolutionary tactic to counter a landscape lacking in the concealment properties of lush, thick forests. The black squirrels in this area could fly, seemingly, but more glided the wind currents to traverse the landscape. The squirrel had fallen from the cottonwood, as was wanting to happen upon the moment of death, but in this case the landing spot happened to be the head which also greeted the sun's rays in an unlikely and odd coincidence of unusual nature.

"Chomp ... chomp ... rip ... rriipp ... ," sounds emanated greedily from the head's mouth. The rest of the head's body remained in place below ground. Only the head was busy.

"Adam Lincoln" was the name carved into the gravestone as a noble identifier of the chomping head's origin. Mr. Lincoln had been the owner of the land and the farmhouse, and the barn and silo on the other side of the hill, as guarded by the cottonwood. The teeth chomps of Mr. Lincoln were steady and determined.

The grass had sprung too high at the bottom of the gravestone bed to see symbols for date of death.

Squirrels resided halfway up the lone, tall tree close behind the tombstone. Nocturnal in nature, the bone snaps and crunches sound awakened in them a vengeance. They scurried away from the chomping sound to reconnoiter. Some of the squirrels clawed their way up and down the tree trunk. They heard Adam Lincoln's mouth break squirrel bones and tear joint tissue a bit too much for their liking. Revenge was now in play for the squirrel pack as Adam's head continued chomping voraciously on the squirrel remains. He then belched, almost rhythmically. He seemed to like the sound. The squirrel pack wasn't stirred into a similar rejoice mode as their interpretation of the sound had become the tripped switch for retribution.

"Mmm…mmm…ooogggg…eeeeegggg … ," Adam's head gurgled out further.

His head remained poked out of the ground from the neck up. Squirrel parts like fur, limb parts and tail remnants were stuck into and between his yellowed teeth. The sordid squirrel meal remains dangled from Adam's lips and mouth, or what was left of a mouth, like beads on a necklace. His lips were tattered and somewhat cracked. What remained of the upper and lower mouth cavity was more a memory, as if it reflected the torn edge of a baloney slice. Teeth were comfortably visible from top to bottom where what remained of full, thin lips previously existed.

Adam Lincoln tested the open air audibly once again in a deep sucking sound of breath. Some wood chips from the coffin still hidden under the ground adorned his dark matted hair. Some facial hair remained on each side of his jaws in the way ivy crawled along tree limbs.

"West Kansas squirrel on a glorious morn; that's good eatin'. Now for some of that fresh beef!" He sniffed the educated sniff of a farmer and was still able to determine a sweet aroma, although his body had been under the ground surface for a year, to the day. The breakfast had heightened his voice inflection capacity.

The immediate squirrel family and cousins, now angered more so, still clung to the tree trunk and limbs which rose upward and outward to the sky from behind the gravestone in the fashion of the Cathedral of Notre Dame. The squirrels looked down upon Adam Lincoln's head, seemed to plot a revenge, as they sounded out a dissatisfaction of sound equal to Adam's temporarily satisfied appetite. It was the only kind of appetite for a Zombie; an appetite voracious and never satisfied; an appetite as regular as the chomps of the cows in the far field methodically ripping and tearing at the grass.

"Chee-chee, chee-chee, gggrrrr, errrggg, chee-chee … ," the squirrel clan snarled.

Zombie Adam Lincoln displayed a panicked look on his weathered face. He tried to remove himself from the grave, but to no avail. He couldn't lift his shoulders and arms above the ground. The squirrel family still worked on a plot to unleash a vengeful attack upon Adam's visible head and a small portion of his neck. The key to every Zombie's survival was to eat "them" or "it" fast, and then move on faster. A reprisal, however, seemed in order from the squirrel clan's view. An increasing tension verbally expressed by the squirrel chatter alarmed Adam.

"What's that? What's that?" He vainly tried to interpret the chatter. He had garnered some experience at learning the chatter language as a regular late afternoon nap under the same tree marked out the years of his life all too frequently, particularly when the harvest results lacked expectation, especially as was the case in the last few seasons of his life, given the bad seed he had purchased and sowed.

The angry squirrel family, no longer obliged to contain itself, descended in attack. They jumped, or rather, parachuted in unison from the tree and sailed the wind in a circular motion, like crows, towards the head of Adam Lincoln. Some landed on the top of the grayed, tilted gravestone. The demon squirrels clawed and dug in, but the marble surface of the stone didn't yield. Some of the squirrel squadron flew past the gravestone and landed on the ground or on Adam's head. Dirt and ripped clumps of grass whirled around Adam's face.

"Whoosh ... rriipp ...clack...clack...clack... rriiippp," drippy sounds swirled in the wind.

Adam screamed, "Aaaahhhh!"

The squirrels retreated briefly at the shrill screech soundings from the Zombie head of Adam, but after regrouping increased the intensity of the attack as they clawed at Adam's head.

"Aaaahhhh! Aaaahhhh! Get off me! Get off me! I'm not beef!"

A young woman named Lilly, about age 23, the still living daughter of Adam, could be seen in the distance as she walked over the hill from behind the tree and down the dirt path; seen and sensed both by Adam and the crazed squirrel mobs. Lilly graduated from law school after completing her undergraduate credits in three and a half years as she worked on her studies throughout the summer breaks, although she was yet to test her mettle in a courtroom except in a clinical study for credit in her last year of law school. During the clinical study she encountered some of the local attorneys in the County of jurisdiction that included her father's farm. She passed the State Bar Exam on her first try but had yet to practice law. The untimely death of her mom Eve and dad Adam caused her to direct much of her energy to keeping up the farm, helped by her brother, Cain, who aspired to become a medical doctor and had completed two years of an internship at a local hospital.

Lilly was beautiful, in the common physical sense of the time, as characterized by her lean, DaVinci curved, busty figure. Today's fashion pleasure consisted of an adornment of beige shorts cropped and cuffed at mid-thigh, a red half halter top, long blonde hair. She wore brown work boots on her feet due to the rough terrain. Her steps kicked up particles of dirt as visible as the stars on a dark clear night. Early morning Sun rays beamed upon the dirt path. Last week's mud streaks adorned the boots as the medallions of life on a farm.

The young Lilly moved closer to the cottonwood tree and gravesite area unaware of the commotion at first, then not long after, aware and frightened as the sea of squirrel dissension washed hard upon her ears. She shrieked when she reached the spot beyond the tree trunk area and spied some of the squirrels torn apart and some still biting and scratching at the head and face of Adam Lincoln's head which still stuck out of the holy ground in front of the gravestone. She could only shriek as the incomprehensible scene darted into her vision.

"Daddy! Daddy! No, you mean critters! Daddy, they dug you up!"

Lilly and Adam unexpectedly communicated in the human realm; unexpected because he was dead and Lilly had only expected, during her walk from the house towards the cottonwood tree, to communicate in an ephemeral, prayer-like sense after laying some flowers down at the gravestone. The squirrels were still attacking Adam's head and face like demons wronged. Adam spotted his daughter's approach when she stumbled in front of Adam's rotted head and facial remains. At first, he didn't seem to recognize her, but then he shouted, as best he could as he tried to muster the use of a partially rotted tongue that flapped like the torn sail of a sea bound skiff. A new mastery of the muscular tentacle awaited future practice.

"Lithely!" Adam sounded out.

Lilly started to go wobbly in the legs when she heard her dead father's head speak. She had seen dead calf's still-born, dead pigs post slaughter, the dead of other small farm species like rats, mice, but never a dead human other than her mom and dad a year ago. She dropped the orange and pink butterfly weed she had picked at first morn from the side garden at the farmhouse and clutched in a tight sweat of a hand on the walk up the hill and over to the family graveyard. A turkey vulture soared well overhead of the scene, patiently awaiting the final curtain call before breakfasting on the squirrel remains.

"Daddy?" Lilly somehow stayed conscious and kicked out at the squirrels. She sent them flying. Some of them slapped against the tree trunk. Some of the squirrels still on Adam's face and head partially dislodged his left eyeball and tore out a clump of Adam's hair and part of his scalp over the right eye. The eye hung limp as a crowded hung Christmas tree ornament.

"KLUG! KLUG! KLUG!"

Lilly, still distraught, shouted some more as a means of excising her grief and anger.

"There! There! There!"

Proceeding from each shout of "There ", a squirrel or two flew outward, spinning away at the impact of Lilly's boot kick. The remaining squirrels were sprayed against the thick cottonwood tree trunk and broke the morning solitude further as they impacted it.

"KLUG! KLUG!"

"There! There!" Lilly shouted some more.

T. S. Eliot would have been proud as the world became a lesser place for some in the rabid squirrel horde. Lilly fainted after the last kick. Falling in a slump downwards, her head faced forward towards her dad's death mask of a look, as she tilted and flopped backwards over the topsoil layer of his grave. They were now face to face, but she was unconscious.

"KLAP." Adam tried to sling a curse, but his tongue mastery still eluded a best, angered effort. He couldn't see Lilly too well because of the one partially dislodged eyeball.

"Oh Lithely, honey. So good to see you. Oh, right, I'm dead, and you're not."

Adam's nose started twitching. His teeth started a biting motion in the air in front of him. His head couldn't reach his daughter's face. His teeth clicked uncontrollably.

"Click … click … click … click." Adam, irritated and frustrated, then verbally castigated himself. "Clap, old man. She's your daughter. Clap, clap, clap, crap...crap. So hungry... ."

Lilly awakened. She saw and heard her father's teeth clicking.

"Click … click … click … click."

Lilly slowly raised up, her pleasantly plump buttocks stretching the beige shorts as she stood. The rest of her torso gradually raised from a triangular position. Between her opened legs, as she looked down on Adam's head still sticking out of the grave, a long stare consumed her solemn face.

"Be right back Daddy," she whispered.

"Where you going?"

"Don't worry. Be right back."

She ran headlong over the hill as she sprayed dirt clumps and grass shards from her boots. The remaining extended squirrel family looked down upon the bizarre scene of chaos below, from a station midway up the tree trunk. Adam looked up at the chattering critters. He still wondered where Lilly was going. The squirrels chirped insults at Adam as they tossed down loose tree branches and seeds which mercilessly pelted his still only exposed head and neck.

To the wind, he questioned, "Can you get me outta here? Lovely weather we are having." Adam looked up again at the squirrels in the tree.

"Darned squirrels. A man's gotta eat! Even a dead one."

Lilly returned with a time-worn banged up and impact scarred white football helmet, duct tape, an old rag and a shovel. "This ought a do it."

"Don't get too close. Click ... click ... ," Adam chanted. First, Lilly duct-taped Adams mouth closed.

"I love you daddy."

"M mm mmm," Adam mumbled.

"I love you too," Adam thought again. Lilly used a rag to push back into the socket the still dangling eyeball.

"That's better. Last year's tornado didn't do you in after all."

"Mmmmm mmm," Adam mumbled into the sticky part of the duct tape. "Thank you," he thought to himself.

Lilly rolled back Adam's scalp and hair and parked the helmet on Adam's head so he couldn't bite her.

"Much better. I am so glad you came back."

Lilly started to dig out the dirt from the grave. She asked a question.

"Did mommy come back too?"

Adam Lincoln looked to his left at the gravestone next to his. A single tear or maybe a long-distance bomb of squirrel pee that hit the mark, ran down his good eye side, along his cheek, as he noticed no movement in or on the ground at the gravestone chiseled with the name, "Eve Lincoln".

Lilly, still full of youthful innocence, despite a scouring pad edge of educational feats, verbally gushed to herself.

"I knew that tornado last year wouldn't do them in."

Lilly dug down carefully into the soil. Adam's teeth incessantly clicked into the tape. Lilly at first was distracted by the continuous clicking. She wondered if it would ever stop. She noticed it became faster and louder as she drew her body closer to the sound. When she backed away, it stopped. She moved towards Adam's face and then back away to judge when the clicking teeth would stop. She dug and dug into the grave area, abusing the usefulness of the shovel, but carefully as she didn't want to tear the flesh from Adam's body. Adam tried to push himself up from the dirt, but his hands kept boring through the loose edges of the grave. Lilly finally reached the point where Adam's waist was visible. The duct tape finally broke apart like a pants zipper.

"I got it from here," Adam blurted out.

He started cupping his hands and swinging his arms like a Ferris wheel ride. West Kansas dirt flew everywhere.

"Here we go, here we go," Adam droned methodically.

Lilly backed away, dropped the shovel metal point down into the soil as she stepped back. The shovel rod and handle stood erect like a post marker. Lilly continued to back away as dirt flew all around her. She raised her arm to her forehead and across her eyes to shield them from the onslaught.

Adam grunted and groaned, moved his head left and right, spied more dirt to cup and throw as he sought the moment, the opportunity, the fateful break when he could free himself. The squirrels looked down upon the football helmet covered head. One of them dropped a large twig down at him. It banged off his helmet. The branch shattered, added to the dirt storm a measure of tree bark shards and strands of cellulose innards. A dirt wall now surrounded Adam on three sides, except the front of him where he faced Lilly.

"Stop! Stop!" Lilly shouted at him. "I think that's enough."

Lilly watched as Adam continued to frantically dig, as if he forgot the purpose was to extricate himself from the grave. Suddenly, Lilly and Adam could hear a loud moaning sound. Each became frozen as their ears attempted to ascertain the origin of the rumbling sound. Adam looked down, and Lilly looked down, at Adam's stomach. His stomach heaved, quivered. Some sinew shook like a rag doll as it poked out like spaghetti strands from his skin.

"I'm hungry!" Adam bellowed.

The squirrels were surprised by the sound of Adam's hungry voice. It was a sound their species hadn't heard from any mammal, avian or insect creature. They scurried to a higher point in the tree. Adam heard their movements against the tree trunk. He looked up. His cold eyes stared them down into a submissive state. The squirrel clan uniformly felt the stare beams crash into their body. They tried to shake them off, but Adam's vision focused intently on them. He reached his hands up towards them, imagined he grasped them and bit their skin, and ripped their limbs off, like humans tore meat from chicken and turkey bones while sinking teeth deep accompanied by twisted grabby, greased fingers pressed hard into the skin and meat and bone.

Lilly backed off. She remembered Adam's quick temper; a bit

harsh at times when he was still alive. His death had not freed him from the accursed ailment. She looked at the shovel to her right still spiked firm into the ground. She reached with both arms towards it, started rocking it back and forth to extricate it from the dirt. When she popped it out, dirt sprayed forth, some into Adam's face, some clicked off the plastic football helmet which still covered his head like a regal crown. The alive squirrels somewhat soured on the assault mission, but the dead ones now infected by Adam's bites, had other ideas.

The dead squirrels around him, some under the recently extricated grave dirt, started moving, they started crawling, scraped what was left of their bodies towards him, except the bodies that had no heads could not easily find their way. Adam enjoyed those squirrel brains earlier. Lilly now regripped the shovel handle. She raised it and started smashing down on the wriggling undead squirrels.

"Daddy, the squirrels are resurrected." Lilly looked in disbelief.

"Watch your voice there," Adam scorned, "We don't need any blasphemy."

Lilly was confused. "But YOU are resurrected."

Adam himself now spread a look of confusion upon his face as wide as a twin-sized frame bedspread. He wondered how he could be alive again.

"Re-, regenerated. Yeths, that's it." Adam's voice resonated.

Adam's jaw adjusted for his next auditory effort, "Let's not bring the wrath of heaven upon us in this hour of my rebirth, please."

Lilly noticed something flying in the air. It alighted upon Adam's left shoulder but before so, Adam noticed the same. It was a ladybug. Lilly remarked to herself, "How pretty." Adam then ejected his tongue and sucked it into his mouth, like a copperhead snake. Another morsel of food since burial a year ago, right after a fresh squirrel's main course.

"MMMMM," Adam moaned.

Lilly was at first shocked. "Dad, you ate a ladybug."

"Yeths, I did. So good. Like a red and black dotted pea."

"Dad. How are you still alive?"

"I don't know, little one. I don't know."

Lilly turned the shovel around and presented it handle end first to Adam. He grabbed it with his right hand. Gnarled and skin torn as it was, he still managed a steady, strong grip. Lilly pulled, used both hands, from the other end of the shovel. Adam slowly emerged from the half dug out grave.

"Keep pulling, girl."

"Ahhh ... ," Lilly grunted as she pulled and pulled some more.

Adam's lower half of body slowly emerged from the dirt, like a worm bored through a detached dead tree limb on the baptism of a rainy morning. He was escaped from his earth sodden home, finally. He laid prostrate on the ground; his hand still clenched to the shovel handle tightly. Lilly fell back slowly and sat in front of him, still holding the business end of the shovel. Each had become lost in mystical thoughts. Their voices then became one.

"Truly, truly, I say to you, an hour is coming and now is, when the dead will hear the voice of the Son of God, and those who hear will live. John 5:25."

They smiled at each other.

"Resurrected you say?" Adam asked Lilly.

"Reborn." She answered. Then she took in a deep breath to allow the strain of the ordeal a soothing release during an exhale from her body. Adam tried to copy her action, but not much movement happened in his chest cavity, almost as if it was frozen into place.

"Whew!" Lilly's hand darted back and forth like a hummingbird just below her scrunched up nose to ward off the smell of dead flesh and rot of body organs. "You need a good dose of baby powder."

Adam sniffed the air, then chuckled. "Sorry. Couldn't imagine what you mean."

The squirrels resumed the ever-present search for food, high up in the tree. Their witness to the birth of a new species fell unimpressive upon any conscience they may have developed over millions of years. Food search and consumption was their only goal. Procreation, an important yet unimpressive after thought in the brave new world cast below them, deposited no need in their thoughts at this time. Consumption, mastication, digestion were the only acts of their mind, in their primeval sensibility. They were witness to the consumption of the human body by the soil and its contents, and to the procreation of a dead man into an undead live man, the two acts now joined as one and the same, yet the squirrels were unimpressed in the West Kansas irony of it all, grimly unaware of the miracle's origin: a bad seed, grown into a bad grain, from which sprung an undead life. The squirrels had seen the worst of the first event. There was much more to witness, yet the unknown didn't concern them.

"Glad you didn't have me embalmed," Adam slurred out.

"Well ... we didn't have much of a choice, given the tornado damages." Lilly's voice took on an entranced state in the talking.

"Cain made you a pine box, like you wanted. I guess otherwise you wouldn't be above ground right now."

"That and other mysteries," Adam slurred again. Hunger and confusion became drum beats he couldn't evade. He wanted to smash the drums like pumpkins.

The last cock trumpeted a call into the bizarre morning's ether. The business of the known sustained them up till now; up till now, alone. There was much more music to blare and much more nuance to learn after the final trumpet sound died into the wind. What about Eve? Was it now the time for the dead to make a new life; etch it out of the West Kansas ground on a mystical path, as travelers to a destination called Unknown? There once was never, and forever now never will ever be.

Adam almost hated himself for such thoughts. He could never speak them. Didn't want to look or sound stupid or become persecuted by the grammar Nazi's. He tried to remain calm, as he knew the eggheads in the squirrel clan, who had not yet been toothily converted into dead meat, would become triggered by his dialect. Selwyn Birchwood's tune, "Even the Saved Needs Saving", blared from a long distance away.

"Nice music sound," Adam remarked.

"Cain restoring another car in the barn," Lilly offered.

Chapter Three

Lilly and Adam methodically lurched onward in a walk back to the farmhouse at a caterpillar's pace. A hurry was not in order. Only a slow march, one tiny step at a time, would suffice for now. The goal was to get Adam into the house and into bed. Along the trek, Adam's tongue could not stop stabbing at flies that hovered too close to his agape mouth. They, including flies, crookedly ambled up the wooden front porch steps, when Adam saw the dreamcatcher waving in the wind. The dreamcatcher Eve had given him as a means to brighten his spirits during the turmoil of the bad seed results wracked upon him, his family, his livelihood.

Cain, Adam's son, the elder of his two children, worked in the garage, fixing a tractor, hood up. He was on break from his studies in medical school. Lilly barked out a General's command just before battle, "Cain!"

The muffled sounds of dropped metal tools against pressed hard dirt preceded the entrance of a young male, just a few years older than Lilly. He was half a foot taller than Lilly, lean as a Bur oak sapling, yet every inch of him rippled of muscle and sinew developed and honed from the work of the farm.

On the trek back to the farmhouse, Adam's mind was tortured by memories of the fateful tornado, the one that took his life and his wife's life, just one year ago. His repeated visions of a flying bandsaw cutting in a swirl through Eve, at her waist, then halved her, splayed her across the West Kansas plain, stung his rotted brain like a migraine from Hades itself. He had crawled against the wind to reach her after the horror presented itself. He could not let her die, he would not let her die, but the wind threw back her gasps, reached into her and into him like octopus tentacles, choked each, until neither could exhale, until breathing had become an impossibility, and death a reality. The wind pounded like a freight train into them, scattered each and the still connected parts of their limbs in all directions. A sweet, familiar human voice pulled him from the phantoms of horrid memory.

"Where did you get that feed for the crops?" Lilly asked Adam.

"Got it from the back of the meat plant. Abel gave it to me cheap, to help us out."

"Gave it to you? Abel doesn't give anything to anybody."

"I don't know. It was pennies on the dollar. Abel said it was special stuff, helped grow crops quicker. Had something in it, some absinthe ingredients and other stuff."

"Absinthe … hummm … what other stuff?"

"I don't remember. Something about Miss Pearl's hand. Magic maybe?"

Cain reminded Adam that Abel worked for Miss Pearl who coveted complete control of Meadow City and the surrounding counties which included the farms. "Miss Pearl?" Adam started to recollect her name, but the meaning of it still eluded capture. "Yes." Lilly added. Then long silence ensued; a time bend which allowed Adam to remember. Thoughts like a cannon ball barrage burst over, around and deep inside him. The memories captured him. Miss Pearl had been trying to buy out the Lincoln's land for years as she wanted to control the crop yields for miles around and he, Adam, remained one of the few holdouts during the land grabs. Good fortune seemed to migrate Miss Pearl's way, Adam recollected when another cannon ball memory exploded, as if Miss Pearl had willed it so. She was the matriarch of a family that controlled nearly the whole County, from the Town leaders to the Court system, either by infiltration of the government system through pre-meditated actions of her kin and kind, or by simple coaxing of the resident landowners' desperate need for cash: many plates of bribery served steamy hot. She maintained a healthy marijuana crop on the side which helped her control even the law system of Sheriff's who served as minions for the trade in exchange for a fair take in the monetary haul. The mindset in and around most of the County was as woeful as the sound of Samuel Barber's "Adagio for Strings".

"It's all starting to come back to me, my memory, in bits and pieces. Anything else I should know?" Adam scratched the side of his face; flaked off some skin shards and dirt.

Lilly and Cain looked at each other, then towards Adam. Each responded in a bit of emphatic "No" manner. Adam scrunched his eyelids down, over wrought-like, which meant he wasn't convinced. Lilly and Cain remained stone-faced in expression. They knew their father was not agreeable to any uncertainty in the meaning of their response. They each knew it was not quite comprehensible to him just yet, which meant he would mentally chew on this "No" for a good bit of time until he could make sense of it. As circumstances would eventually reveal, his son and daughter knew Adam would finish chewing on the thought, over a good bit of time, until he was ready to spit out the meaning to each of them. For now, the mid-summer leaves started to tint brown in preparation for their graceful autumn dance in a race of time against Adam's skin shards.

Chapter Four

Lilly drove her father Adam Lincoln into Meadow City, in the pickup truck. Wrapped in a dark green tarp to help mask the smell of dead flesh, Adam sniffed and snorted. At home, he had changed clothes from his plain black burial suit into a dark hoody, overalls, and work boots. Most of the townspeople may not have noticed his aroma amidst the cattle butchering Plant machinations nearby. As the truck approached the town like a suspicious dog, a visibly irritated protest group crowded Main Street. Protestors held up signs like badges. The signs splayed the West Kansas wind of minced words like "Social Justice Now".

Adam asked, "What's social justice now?"

Lilly tried to find a lawyerly explanation, abandoned the effort, then reconsidered and blurted out, "Meatloaf. It's meatloaf."

"Yum," Adam intoned, his single, distinct syllable muffled through the tarp. He exhaled a chuckle which sounded out more like a cough.

"Looks like college kids," Lilly observed.

"They dress kind of funny," Adam uttered. His head rotated in a loose swivel from side to side to focus and gather full meaning of the group. The irritated street crowd hailed from the local college, apparently using the town as practice for bigger and better tantrum episodes in the larger, more populace areas of the conventional citizenry. Adam was hungry for live flesh;

eternally hungry. An older, gray-bearded man in the crowd, assisted by a tightly gripped bull horn in one hand, shouted out protest slogans.

"What do we want?"

"Justice!" The crowd whined.

The bull horn playing man seemed encouraged.

"When do we want it?"

"Now!"

Adam's hunger refused to wane.

"Meat, we want meat, now," Adam mumbled.

Lilly had to stop the truck, surrounded by still shouting, angry protestors who spouted as if no one could hear them. Even the birds on the tree limbs and telephone pole wires seemed irritated by the orated racket. The protestors banged on the sides of the truck applying fists and protest signs and slapped on the partially rolled down windows. Some of them looked like Zombies, but they were not. Lilly ventured an observation.

"I think some of them are high," Lilly noted, "not Zombies". Then she stopped verbal observation as she feared Adam may start to consider some unpleasant thoughts.

"That bull horn rooster is eggin' them on," Adam blurted out.

Then he tried to add some levity to the strained situation. "What? I thought we were in the car wash."

Lilly's face became tensed by the protestors. Adam tried to figure her meaning. "Probably got a hold of some of Miss Pearl's wacky weed."

"You mean Mary Jane?" Lilly asked. "Dad, they don't call it that anymore, not for a long time. And it's considered medicine now."

"Don't forget to get some while we're here."

"Dad!"

"What?"

"I am trying to get a job with a law firm."

"Oh. Boy, it sure was a good idea for me to buy that life insurance policy for me and your mom."

"Only thing keeping us going, and stalling Miss Pearl's greedy advances on the farm," Lilly added.

"I thought Miss Pearl was trying to help the families." Adam observed.

"No Dad. Turns out she was trying to run them out of the County after taking their land," Lilly advised, as she dreaded when at a future time, she would have to update Adam on details of the

Witch coven activities across the County and Meadow City.

"Bitch," Adam punctuated the point further. Then he tossed in for good measure another thought. "These college kids sure can make a racket. Wish we could make them vanish."

"Funny, Dad. You know, there's a rumor around town that Miss Pearl is a Witch, and not just that, the leader of a Witch coven."

Adam thought for a bit. He wondered how he could have missed such an observation about Miss Pearl.

"No kidding. Pretty scary. I always thought she was a good Witch, as in personality, not in profession." Then he directed a few more prescient sentiments for Lilly to chew on.

"Don't forget to buy some weed from these clowns before we get back, you know, for medicinal purposes. I did just come back from the dead you know. The bones and muscles are still a bit creaky."

"Sure, Dad."

"Oh. Get me a pint of that Narcissist ice cream."

"The what kind of ice cream?"

"Narcissist. You know, the kind made by Bert and Ernie. Makes you feel good, then feels like it stabs you in the back as it's going down the throat. Gives a good brain freeze. That ice cream has a mind of its own. The container, in the freezer, invites another eater to feast upon it. I always considered it the "adulterer" ice cream. Always got the sloppy seconds, it seemed."

"You okay, Dad?"

"Yes. Yes, I am. Anyway, your mother used to like it much."

"If you only knew." Lilly mumbled.

"What?" Adam asked.

"Nothing, Dad. Nothing."

Adam darted at her the look of "you know what I mean". Lilly understood, but scrunched up one side of her face as if confused.

Someone had clicked on the radio in the grocery store and it now rained the musical mist of Wynonie Harris bellowing, "Shake That Thing".

"We'll see, Dad. We'll see."

The crowd still pushed against the truck windows. Lilly just looked for a parking space as her intention was to buy some fresh meat at the local grocery store, at Adam's request. The meat in Kansas had more flavor than other places because it was fresher, straight from the slaughterhouse to the grocery store. Lilly tried not to hit any of the crowd clowns, but they barked and screamed at her in faux pain fashion anyway. She parked, still surrounded by protesters who pounded on the truck body using fists, shoes, wooden sign poles. She exited and pushed her way towards the grocery store. The protestors continued their rant, sometimes screaming obscenities at a fever pitch. Someone in the unruly crowd threw a rock and it broke the truncated passenger window of the truck. The glass shards found their way into Adam's clothing.

"What a hero. More like a Nero," Adam told himself. "Who's the goofball with the ponytail?" Adam asked.

Lilly sarcastically shouted back, "He's a professor at Community College of Wokeville, a few towns over." Then she became lost to Adam's hearing as she entered the grocery store. Adam exited the truck, escaped from the tarp to stretch his muscles, ligaments and activate the rustic bones which held him up even in the undead state. The hoody guarded his face, mostly.

The professor protest leader, a long-haired, bandana-clad fifty something in age riot monger, who seemed to like his own voice, decided Adam would make a good example, so professor barked instructions through a bullhorn to the youthful, college aged crowd to pull Adam away from the truck. The protest mongers carried him forward and placed him in front of the professor protest leader, all the while beating upon Adam using wooden sticks from handwritten signs adorned by peace symbols and nonsensical political curses. Adam's hunger now reached a fever pitch as he slowly and steadily brushed off glass shards from the broken truck window.

One of the protesting youths shouted, "Wow he's ripe," as the protestor danced a hand just below his own narrow nose. Adam mumbled, "You look ripe, too, friend."

The old hippy professor, as Adam saw him, vomited all manner of political dogma against mythical enemies of the people. Adam started to think a bit, despite his voracious physical hunger pangs. This old hippy was feeding the flaccid minds of the young ones a bunch of bullshit so he could feel better about himself. The old hippy didn't give a rat's ass what happened to anyone else. He started haranguing on about Adam, a farmer drone, and his family hive. As best as Adam could tell, he never met the hippy man, never knew him or his kin, so Adam was at a loss about how he and his own family could be treated so poorly, bad-mouthed by an old fart who he had never met. The more the hippy ranted, the more he looked like cattle to Adam. Adam stepped closer to the hippy professor, sniffed him. "Meat," Adam thought. The hippy man was riled up in such a frothy frenzy, he didn't notice the degree temperament of Adam's appetite face. Some in the crowd threw tomatoes at Adam. He didn't even duck. The tomatoes cracked on impact against Adam's head and back and split and spewed juices onto the hippy professor's shirt and neck area.

Adam coughed out, "Limp dicks." The crowd remained oblivious to his sounds as they ate up the hippy leader's syllables like teaspoons of Gerber's baby food. Adam tried to remember the faces of the vegetable throwers, as they had, in his mind, put themselves on his edible menu. During this entire time, Adam still cowered inside his clothing of overalls and a dark hoody pulled almost completely around his face. The protestors didn't know what was coming, which is how things worked in Western Kansas for strangers, be it a stealth tornado or crunching hailstorm or unmerciful wind shear. In the current situation, Adam imagined the newspaper would call it something regal like the "Adam Event" in the top of the fold headline, but not really, because no one would expect he had come back to life. His work boots would do nicely as a weapon of choice. A deft kick to the groin and the selected offender in the crowd would have fallen like a ton of bricks; but the target now, in Adam's current state, was the neck, and the veins on the old hippy prof's neck as they were busting out, readied to be chomped, begging greedy and gleefully to be drained, in Adam's perspective. Oddball hippy prof's neck veins wriggled like earthworms in a plastic sandwich bag waiting to be dug out and pricked upon a fishhook.

Adam heard a scream. He looked over at the grocery store. Some of the college protestors started to push up against Lilly as she left the grocery store with a big brown bag of meat products. Adam could smell every brand and type of meat in the rippling bag. The bag ripped and the meat started to fall out. One of the protestors used a wooden pole and clunked Lilly in the head. She raised up her arms after the impact and pulled the pole. The protestor went flying down into the wooden porch step. The others started to swarm like fire ants. Adam had enough. He looked over at the frothy-faced old hippy prof, then Adam opened wide, flexed his jowls like that of a great white shark, rolled his eyes back until they looked like shiny golf balls, and bit the jeering hippy deep into the neck at the point of the squirming bulgy vein, just as old hippy man was shouting another expletive. Then Adam pulled back the bite, severed the neck flesh in a gooey clump and took the vein harbored in it. Blood squirted everywhere like a popped water balloon.

The angry protestors were now frenzied, panicked prey for Adam. As he sucked down the fresh blood like a half-melted grilled cheese sandwich, he leapt onto the crowd and started clicking methodically his jaws into anything that moved. One of the protestors objected to Adam's assaults.

"Hey! You can't do that! It's a free country!"

Adam searched for a smart-ass answer, then found one. "Yes, it is. Here are your freedoms today: police cruiser, hospital bed, Medical Examiner's exam table. On that last one, bring a sweater or jacket."

The protestor zipped out like a rabbit; everywhere and nowhere, screamed, "Mama, mama!".

"I ate her yesterday," Adam laughed out between syllables. "Not even worth the effort," he then snorted blood droplets. Gnats scattered away from the red rain.

The crowd broke ranks and started running away in all directions, but not before Adam collected a few chunks of sweatshirt, arm flesh, leg bone, from varied and random college kid ravers. Lilly had pummeled and kicked her way out of the rows of crowd corn until she had cleared a path over to Adam.

"Dad, you okay?"

"Much better." Then he added, "Watch out for some of these butt barnacles laying on the ground. I took some chunks out of them. Don't know if they will wake up human or Zombie, if they wake up, you know, like in the comic books and TV shows type stuff."

"Dad, some egghead got into the truck. I am sorry. I left the keys in it out of habit."

They each recognized the familiar sound of the old cylinders cranking and banging under the truck hood, then looked over at where it was parked and saw it spinning wheels and flinging dust and variously racing away amidst the crowd chaos.

"Lilly, is that old bald tire still on the front right of the truck?"

"Yes."

Then they heard a pop sound and watched as the truck skidded into a gasoline tank at the corner gas station. As the gasoline oozed out of the dislodged hose handle, it streamed under the truck and the fumes caught fire from the heated engine. The flames spread high and quick.

"Wow! Barbecue too!" Adam couldn't contain himself. He tried out an air sniff, but his nose rejected the effort.

"Dad, you really know how to make the most of a moment, even in death ... or ... after death."

"Whatever, hon. I prefer the term 'unlife', if you don't mind."

"Now what?" They each asked out loud at the same time. The scene appeared reminiscent of a Revelations apocalypse.

"I think we need to figure this out with Cain's help. That medical school son of mine is a pretty smart one, like his mom."

"I won't take that as an insult." Lilly laughed.

"None given, my future District Attorney." Adam felt bad he had slighted her praise. Then he added, as he always wanted to put in the last word, "Oh, and mind the need for wacky weed. Seems to be bags of it scattered around all over. Those college kids got spooked out of their own highs."

"Daddy, after all of this fiasco, I'm not sure what is worse, old hippy college professors, Witches, or your so-called wacky weed."

Adam thought as best he could think about the situation. "I'd put my money on the wacky weed. Medicinal purposes, you know. Seems college professors and their school kids are a bit wacky, even without the weed. As for Witches, they aren't all bad."

Chapter Five

Once back at the farm, the afternoon dictated a scheduled sit on the front porch as a necessary arrangement and so commenced in kind. Adam leaned back in the lone rocking chair and Cain in the Flanders wicker armchair. For a long time, a stillness reigned; a solemn quiet; the moments solace craved. A cool wind accompanied and comforted them. Adam looked out upon his land. A dreary sight it was; a smeared up, foggy mirror of chaos even a light West Kansas wind couldn't reconcile. Adam spoke.

"You thinkin' 'bout cars again?"

"Sure, sure Dad," Cain answered.

Rocking chair creaks bent across old but strong wood planks, serenaded by peeled paint strips as they danced, aided by the wind, along the porch floor.

Faint tinkles of glassware split into the kitchen's air from behind them. The spitted tinkles grew silent as a soft liquid tea lip-lip-lipped into the bottom of a glass, then hugged coolly against rounded smooth insides. Careful soft footsteps approached Adam and Cain from behind.

"Got a story Dad?" Cain asked in a slow, expectant tone.

"Sure, I do. Porch philosophy, my past-time. You know that."

"I know that," Cain rhythmically obliged.

"Remember George Pullman?" Adam asked.

"Sure do," Cain answered, "He's still around. Down the road a way, at his property."

"Good, good. I was hoping so," Adam whispered in a steady manner. "How's George's missus, Edith?"

Cain thought a while before answering. "No one knows. George doesn't talk about it. Some say maybe she left, on account of the things going on, in and around town."

Adam rocked his chair faster. "That's a shame."

Cain waited for Adam to inquire further, but he didn't. Perhaps Adam would see George soon and ask him for the story. Cain offered as a lead question to oblige the beginning part of a different story.

"What do you think George would think about all this coming back to life type stuff?"

"Nice of you to ask, son. Was wondering the same."

Lilly arrived with a cafeteria tray upon which sat three clear glasses of iced tea.

"Thanks, hon," Adam said. Cain nodded a thank you look to Lilly.

"Thanks for picking us up from the chaos in town," Lilly directed to Cain. Cain smiled. Lilly then sat down on the porch near Cain, cross legged, sipped tea and readied herself for Adam's story.

"Yeah, son. You're a life saver." They laughed, nervously.

"Still worried about mom," Lilly stated. Cain nodded.

"Me too, hon," Adam agreed. "We'll go down to the cottonwood tree and check on her. See if she is okay. Bring a shovel and what not, right after this tea," Adam promised. Adam then proceeded to the tell of a story he heard from George Pullman years ago about the meaning of a soulmate.

"George and I had been talkin' about life, like usual, when we happened upon the idea of a soulmate."

Adam said George knew something about this matter. "A soulmate isn't someone who completes you. No, a soulmate is someone who inspires you to complete yourself."

Adam continued the good long think he had started when he first sat down. He reached down in his soul to pluck out a ripe hopper of a story, of the kind that weighs down the brain of the listener, reshapes it, and allows the listener a new life perspective, for use as needed, or waste as discarded, if not useful. Such was the way to politely offer information in this part of West Kansas.

"Found this one on the internet a few years back and kept the paper in my pocket after your mom printed it out for me. I guess it comes from an internet philosopher, so to speak, named Rainbowsalt. Odd sounding name. Not sure how to pronounce it. Thought it might one day prove to have some profound meaning. Seemed all right given our circumstances." Adam pulled out a yellowed piece of paper and began to read.

"A soulmate is someone who does not judge you for your flaws. A soulmate is someone who sees your jagged edges, who sees the parts of you that have been weathered by love and by life, who sees the wars that you fight, and who chooses to stand beside you. A soulmate is someone who watches as you confront your scars from the inside; always encouraging you to heal on your own time, in your own way; always encouraging you to keep going."

"That Rainbowsalt person sounds like a smart one," Cain obliged.

Adam then concluded, "I think your mom, she could have been my soulmate."

At the end of the reading, Cain noticed some movement in the distance. As the movement drew closer, they each speculated about what was in the rustled dry, truncated wheat stalks. Adam posited a dog. Cain speculated a possum. Lilly offered no insight except that she wasn't sure; couldn't tell from the distance between them and the origin of the rustling. Eventually they realized it was Eve, or at least her body top half, as she arm-crawled like a crab across the nearly barren ground. No words could they gather at the sight of her, so silence stood instead to freeze the void of horror and wonder.

This next adventure unfolded itself slowly, amidst a steady wind on the dead West Kansas wheat field. Dark clouds rolled in low over top of the porch from behind the house and across the sky.

A darker sky it became. The yellowed porch light clicked the "On" sound. A gentle rain commenced upon the barren fields; stretched out in front of them. Each wet drop reflected the yellowed porch light, as if a meteor shower had begun. The human crab continued an approach. Adam wondered what George would think of the scene.

Chapter Six

Cain gave Adam a ride, in one of the still-working trucks, on over to George's place.

"Something on the horizon, Dad?" Cain imagined asking Adam; but he didn't ask. He knew. Sometimes questions with known answers served no purpose to pose. Perhaps, to comfort a stirring soul, yes. Maybe, to reassure the ego of the broken, yes. A confident silence served the same purpose.

"Got some questions, for George," Adam whispered.

Cain put his thumb and two fingers on the bill of his cap; adjusted it up and down. A silent confirmation would do, but he could tell something else was on Adam's mind. A bright moon lit the way along the path to George's farm, as the truck neared closer. In the distance, they could see George rocking in a chair on his porch.

Cain pulled up to the edge of the dirt driveway, Adam exited, Cain watched the scene unfold. Adam raised a hand to George. George nodded acceptance of the visit. The truck engine choked a few times. Cain backed up, turned the truck around and slow rolled along the driveway as an energy from deep inside him started a simmer of emotion somewhat comparable in degree to the dust spewed from the truck's rear tires.

Once safely seated on George's front porch in a long-ago vacated wooden rocker, much silence controlled the air. Then the silence fled, and much conversation and idled oratory marched out from each of their syrupy vocal cords. The banter eventually led to George calmly spouting to Adam some wisdom on the matter at hand.

"When the person I trusted the most left me, I started walking into different rooms of the house and thinking, now I am truly alone, but after a while, I realized, I was not alone because I was in the room, with myself. I learned more about myself as I listened to the whispers of those I had encountered throughout my life. Eventually I became comfortable with myself, and now I am on the path of a new life."

Adam tried to catch up to George's words as they escaped meaning for Adam like young deer scared into the high brush. George also related there was a rumor all about in the County, about a war between Witches and Zombies that had commenced, in unavoidable fashion, given the Witches had yet to master a command of spells to quiet the unrest.

"You mean I am not the first Zombie?" Adam asked.

"No, not by a long shot, at least according to the rumors."

George continued to update Adam on the current situation. Miss Pearl was a Witch, and a strong one. Zelda was one of her elite minions, also a Witch, but of somewhat lesser mastery of spells and incantations. Many Witch spells involved infestation and conquest of the soul's mind, yet Zombies apparently had no souls in their present state. Their souls wandered in other realms, just as the Zombies roamed in the earth realm. The connection of soul and mind was severed. Missing the link between each, Witches could only move Zombies like objects, but the link was fuzzy, unreliable, could be severed randomly by an odd sound, sometimes created by the friction of wind against other objects like rocks, trees, land crevices, even the willowy swath of high grass or wheat could alter the spell path or connection. George speculated the Witch clans would eventually figure out a work around to this predicament which impeded their narcissistic obsession for control over all living and unliving things. Except Zombies were a problem to control because they were dead, yet still sentient creatures. Perhaps there was some electrical connection that was short-circuited by the Zombie mind status. George halted explanation to check on Adam.

"You okay, Adam?" George asked.

"It's a bit much, George, but I will try to understand."

George continued verbalizing his beliefs along this vein of thought as he filled in Adam about how the Witch, Miss Pearl, casted spells upon the land and landowners. Some of the magic was wicked pretty. George learned about the scheme from a cousin who did housekeeping chores for money at the one of the Witch residences. The cousin wouldn't say the name of the Witch due to fear her family would be hexed.

George tried to explain magic and Witchcraft to Adam. "Magic involves an illusion. Witchcraft transforms an illusion into reality."

For instance, Miss Pearl and sometimes Miss Zelda used love

potions to help split up husband and wife. One or the other or both would cheat on each other, then after the spell wore off, the Witch would start a rumor about the adultery and cause the spouses to break apart. Some of the adulterers worked for the Witch, so the sexual favors must have been part of their compensation. The financial break would almost always involve selling off the land during the divorce split. The buyer was always someone working for the Witch.

Sometimes a hex was put on the grain which would dry up the crop. Many of the farms suffered such an attack by the Witch clan. Financial ruin followed and no escape was available from the local bankers if they had also been bewitched.

Sometimes a control spell was casted upon certain authorities such as Police, Judges, Real Property Clerks in the courthouse in order to control proceedings and documents to crush the will of the property owners.

Sometimes the weather was controlled and directed to cause havoc and panic. Only the strongest Witches alone, or a coven together in a group could direct such a condition of woe.

Adam then determined to espouse some wisdom he had learned as a farmer and friend to others. "If we are blessed to live long enough to learn this lesson, we begin to realize many who became friends were actually enemies who wanted something from us. Don't get to know other humans to 'make' friends. Live to learn what humanity is about and act according to the convictions that make 'you' comfortable, first and foremost. From this perspective, the blinders will be lifted from your vision, and you will become more adept at identifying the hungry wolves at the gate; lessen the amount and immensity of relationship blunders."

George seemed impressed. He nodded in agreement. "Now you're getting it."

"Those spells, George. Don't know what to do about them."

It was happening. A time was coming, of chaos and woe, Adam thought. Perhaps it was the prelude to making all right and good again, for as long as it could last in this place. He looked to the east and upward, because the moon betrayed an intruder invading its light. An eerie purple haze invaded torn, snaky cloud patches as they reached fingers towards and over the moon's face. The first order of business, for Adam, was Officer Clinton's death. "I need my revenge on Clinton," Adam stated. George looked out towards the fields.

"He's already dead. You'll have to ask Cain about the details." Adam, surprised as a feeling of having been cheated pierced his chest, asked how? When?

"Clinton stopped your son a little while back, not far down the road, apparently to set him up for a drug bust by planting drugs in the car. Cain coaxed Clinton into inspecting the car trunk, then a few Zombies in the car trunk took care of the rest. What's left of Clinton is in the barn."

Adam searched for the right words. "Wow. That's my boy. One less revenge to go."

Chapter Seven

Is there magic in this world? After Adam found Eve, he wanted to help restore her into a whole self, at least physically, to start. She didn't demonstrate any sense of a sentient being. Her only verbalized noise involved random clicks of her mouth against some remaining teeth yet to be pinched by the rot of time. He arranged a visit to his neighbor, Miss Zelda, who was rumored to be a Witch. Adam didn't tell Cain or Lilly about his meeting venture. Adam only knew for certain Miss Zelda worked as the City and adjacent County prosecutor in criminal and civil proceedings. Before leaving, Adam went back to the cottonwood tree and dug up the lower half remains of Eve. There hadn't been much of her left to put into the grave, given the circumstances of death. He carried her lower body half remains back to the farmhouse and placed them around Eve's body in the same old family steamer trunk he used to store her upper body. Her upper body half he had previously laid comfortable on her back. She randomly clicked her teeth when Adam opened the trunk lid. He tried to make her comfortable in a cocoon of wool blankets.

"Eve, I'll do my best, hon, to bring you back. I promise," Adam said. He then closed and latched the lid for her safety.

Miss Zelda reported to Miss Pearl, an elderly woman now, but many generations had known of her as young. The mysterious stories about Miss Pearl had been passed down from generation to generation. Some thought her lineage included a Witch of unknown origin and thereafter each generation carried forth the mission of an ancestral original.

It was rumored a town Elder, in the older times, had determined Miss Pearl to be a Witch when she was noticeably young. It was further rumored Miss Pearl had been scheduled to be burned alive to purify the town called Meadow Village, now known as Meadow City, and to serve as a warning to others of Miss Pearl's kind to stay away. The town's attempted action had the reverse effect. No known record existed of a Witch burning from generations ago. The event only resided in imagination and old tales passed on verbally at community gatherings and such events. More and more nearby villages took root. As old stories go, at least one unique wrinkle to each telling evolved. The result came to be the story of the outer parts of the town and beyond had become ruled by Witches.

The men of the town took offense to the rise of women in power and taunted the only possible cause as Witchcraft. The powerful men used the accusation of the practice as a shield to cloak their own feelings of inadequacy. The resulting social friction never quite subsided but lessened in intensity. The reason for the change never came to light, officially. The most extant rumor indicated Witches eventually came to the area and formed a coven to consolidate power for their own protection. The arrogance of the town leaders had risen so high, they deemed the town a City, although if it stood as such, it was the smallest City around, anywhere. Eventually the Witch influence overtook the area.

Adam vowed to restore Eve's complete body. The only person able to help him would be Ms. Pearl through the means of her dark and powerful magic. Eve was powerless to stop Adam's attempt at a regeneration of the relationship. Her memory didn't seem to take notice of what had been between them, in each of them, for such a long time before it was scattered by the difficult circumstance of the crop failures on their land. The bridge they created to hold the relationship together had broken a long time ago, for them and for most of the other families who stayed in the area where they and their ancestors' imprint on the land and community had been as solid as a cement pavement. Over time, the cement had begun to crack and the imbedded stones to loosen.

After many attempts at communication, Miss Zelda, who was a high-ranking member of the coven and lived near Adam just over the northern ridge of his property, finally made herself available for a meeting in Miss Pearl's stead. As a District Attorney in the local Court system, her power went beyond Witchcraft. She had combined in skill that art and too the art of lawyering, a powerful one-two punch at the face or gut or soul of any adversary. Adam suspected she was fully aware of his predicament as an "undead" person. He had helped spread the rumor of his predicament to offer Miss Zelda a third punch of power, if she could acquire it, in exchange for the meeting. His tactic was almost a dare at her to try and take control of him. His secondary purpose, after help sought for Eve's predicament, was to get close enough to understand Miss Zelda's strengths and weaknesses in order to gain an edge in the conflict which would become inevitable, as he perceived it, between the remaining uncontrolled farmers, the Witches, and the "undead" Zombie community gradually evolving upon the scene.

Adam and George had offered lodging to the known undead at their respective properties. These undead were only sentient in the sense they craved meat. Adam and George didn't at first understand why, but they eventually came to believe the bad seed spread by Abel, Miss Pearl's lackey, only extended into their own properties. George never got around to using the seed. It was still stored in a granary on his property. Adam had used the seed as he was low on good seed supply. The cataclysm for his family played out into the current situation, aided by the mysterious family of tornadoes that regularly visited.

Together, Miss Zelda and Adam sat in a dark parlor off the edge of a main hallway. In the shadows of the room Zelda remained as Adam sat in the midst of a modest and dim table lamp. The chair provided him was uncomfortable, even for an undead. He noticed Zelda rested upright, appeared relaxed, on a loud and puffy soft couch of lush fabric, red in color, ringed on the edges by dark wood animal carvings of a species not familiar to him. The lamp rested next to Adam on a short wooden cabinet adorned by unusual carvings of naked men and women, the bodies of each intertwined in a mysterious and puzzling manner. The table feet were shaped like animal claws, of which type uncertain to Adam.

Miss Zelda spoke first. "So, are you here to admire the furniture, or do you merely seek favor?"

Any pretense of manners evaded Adam in his undead state.

"Neither and both," he stated, steady as room shadow stares.

"You've been dead a year. To catch up on things, are you?" Miss Zelda asked.

"Yes. Yes, that's it. Catch up," Adam agreed.

"Well, I fail to see how you can help me. Just your thought of it is rather bold."

Adam started to become agitated. He wanted to just leap out of the uncomfortable chair, latch onto her, sink his teeth into her shoulder and yank out as much flesh and meat as possible. He sensed Zelda knew such.

"Perhaps you can help me," she said. "Bring me a lock of Miss Pearl's hair. Then we can talk further."

Adam thought for a bit. He realized the predicament. Zelda craved more power. Apparently, the only direction she could maneuver to get it was upward, as most of the prospects below her status had already been exploited. He was glad she didn't ask for his property. Perhaps she assumed it would one day be hers, given his situation of death. Of course, Zelda would not legally need to take it from Adam. She could plot to take it from Lilly and Cain. Adam masked a shudder of angst.

"I need time to plan."

"Granted, but we are mid-summer. All avenues will be closed at the end of summer, for everyone, even the undead."

"Crap," Adam thought, "she already knows about the Zombies I created."

"Understood," Adam stated, but he had no idea what she meant.

"Good."

The meeting ended. Adam stood, started to walk out of the room, but looked back, and saw the puffy soft couch, red in color, was empty, as if no one had been sitting in it at all; not any visible sign of a body's impression of rump or torso against the soft edges revealed themselves. Outside, as the light faded from another day, Adam wondered about the meaning of Miss Zelda's request. Was his task a test of his faith in her? Or did Miss Zelda bear ill intent towards Miss Pearl?

For those who lusted for power above all, Adam knew well that too much power was never deemed enough. Such a capricious lust pressed down like a curse upon those whose appetite could never become satiated. Perhaps he discovered an avenue of defense against the Witch coven arts. A consultation with George Pullman screamed in his head as the necessary order.

PART TWO

Regenerations

Chapter Eight

Lightnin' Hopkins' tune, "Mistreated Blues" motored in unison to an old Buick, almost as if tuned to perform so. Cain tooled down the road in the engine restored '68 Buick Skylark he experimented on for a neighbor, changing speed sounds from purr to whir during the test drive. He was briefly interrupted by a mobile phone call from Lilly regarding the status in town and the loss of Adam's truck. Cain was pissed as he had put in a good bit of time fixing the motor. He started to wonder if God was a psychopathic narcissist.

Lilly then broke the bad news to Cain. Adam had been picked up by Officer Clinton for suspicion of murder committed at the protests in Meadow City. Adam was now housed in the City Jail pending a trial, which was sure to commence in the near future.

"I'll be there in a bit," Cain promised Lilly.

He heard siren sounds, clicked off his mobile phone as red-light beams whirled around and penetrated the Skylark's wide windows. He pulled over to accommodate a hounding by the local Sheriff's Department. The officer exited his government vehicle as the roof lights continued to blare in red sprits. The beams spread out along the ground like tracers from a twirling gun. The officer, gun drawn, walked up to the driver's side.

"Son, let's see your license and registration."

"Oh, hello Officer Clinton. Nice evening."

Cain started to reach over to the glove compartment and the officer yelled, "Stop that!"

"Just doing what you asked," Cain stated.

"You have any weapons?"

"No, so to speak."

"Don't get smart with me boy. I know who you are."

"I know who you are," Cain calmly responded. He knew Clinton was the bag man for Miss Pearl. Clinton collected all the money, land and house deeds from the property owners Miss Pearl forced into bankruptcy or worse, to enrich her western Kansas financial empire. Her means of coercing the transfers ranged from blackmail to morality morose entrapment and even death threats against property owners and kin. Prostitution, illicit drug substances, violence threats blew across the plain as regularly as the uncurtailable Kansas wind. The officer's Cheshire cat smirk turned into a demon scowl.

"Get out!"

"Sure, sure, I'll even pop the trunk lid for you so you can search for the drugs you will claim are in there." As Cain opened the driver's door, he reached down and pulled the trunk release lever. The trunk lid popped up a bit.

"Now you are getting it," the officer audibly smacked back at him.

Cain stood next to the driver's side of the car as the officer holstered his gun, then roughly turned Cain around to face the car, then pulled back Cain's arm's. Clinton unclipped handcuffs from his belt.

The car itself wasn't much. It was old and rusted, but a finely tuned motor performed in the brash manner of a bootlegger's rod. Clinton started the handcuffing process, had clipped one metal claw onto Cain's left hand, and was about to clip the other when a gust of wind, or something, lifted the trunk lid. Clinton snapped his head towards the trunk lid.

"Your piece of crap car needs more than a fancy motor," Clinton rattled out in a smarmy tone.

"Oh, it has much more than that," Cain countered.

"Keep your pie hole shut!"

Clinton's mood, as usual, bordered on the edge of anger, like moss clinging from a pond cypress, greedily searching for another tree branch or trunk to engulf. He had long ago succumbed to ravages of drug addiction related to insidious attempts by Miss Pearl to entrap victims in the cage of shame. As the drug transporter and distributor, Clinton had tested one too many batches to the point of triggering his own addiction. As long as depraved opportunities sparkled and pranced in the embodiment of one of Miss Pearl's blackmailed whores, he couldn't care less.

Clinton was known to provide drugs to women he desired. Eve

fell into the trap and became one of them. Cain counted on such a reaction once the trunk lid popped, as it meant Officer Clinton would barge on over to the rear of the Skylark. As the temper tantrum emerged, the trap had been sprung.

In the dark shadows of the night, driven by an unquenchable thirst to quash any who he confronted, Clinton succumbed to the temptation of creating further mayhem. He walked to the back of the Skylark like a man on a mission. He lifted his hand to hold open wide the lid. Unceremoniously, the wide grin-like choppers of two zombie dead greeted his visage as if it was the main course at the buffet. His face was hopelessly lost on the first munch. All the roundness of his eyeballs, popped from the sockets, started a slow and determined pinball roll into the trunk's dankness. His hands thrashed about for something to grab, but as he was the main course, they were broken off like the limbs of a fresh-cooked Thanksgiving Day turkey, emulating the sounds of such rips. He couldn't even scream, as simultaneously, the second zombie soldier cheated Clinton of the capacity for sound as a throat clamp of teeth and jowl closed the piano lid.

The Zombie works nearly completed, except for the gurgling sounds of difficult digestion, Cain slow walked towards the remains of Officer Clinton, most of which had taken a sullen rest upon the asphalt street bed. After some gymnastic type of physical workings, he was able to remove the handcuff keys from the waist belt of Clinton, and free himself to complete the deed.

"Thanks, gentlemen," Cain said. He found a flashlight strapped to Clinton's belt, pulled it out of the leather pocket, clicked it to "on" and checked his partners in retribution. He apologized.

"Sorry, mam," he said to one of the Zombie munchers. "Hard to see on this night."

A low-level mist began rolling from the woods which abutted the street line. "Guess we better get going before the bullfrogs start a serenade."

Cain picked up the remains of Officer Clinton and tossed them into the trunk, then closed the lid. "Worked out better than I thought."

The throaty groans of the bullfrogs began the exit song. Cain looked up at the moon. "What a pretty night."

His work, however, wasn't finished. Still had to strip Officer Clinton's vehicle. He went back to the Skylark, dialed the mobile phone, and requested help from Lilly. She suggested he call George Pullman. He didn't live far from there. Cain related, "I don't want to bother George. Maybe I can find a place just off the road to hide the police cruiser."

"I'll call George, see if he can hold onto the cruiser for a while until we figure out the rest of the plan," Lilly suggested.

Cain agreed. "Okay, sounds good. I'll head over to George's. Maybe he can give me a ride back so I can pick up the Skylark and our trunk buddies."

Cain wondered briefly whether he should let Lilly know about

Officer Clinton's timely demise, but he relented on the thought.

"Just one more thing. Officer Clinton is dead. He asked me to pop the trunk. Our Zombie friends were hungry."

Lilly cautioned. "Won't be long before Miss Pearl or her minions notice Clinton missing."

"If there's hell to pay, then there's hell to make," Cain responded. "Hay's in the barn, now."

Lilly was confused, "What?"

"Oh, that's something I heard a fella' from Baltimore say once, when I was in town for a medical seminar and took a few drink's at Zeke's Café."

"Ready for hell was Cain's specialty," Lilly thought, almost a bit too much reminiscent of their feisty mom.

"So, Daddy. That's how Officer Clinton died," Lilly stated from her seat in a folding metal chair.

On his back, Adam rested. Stretched out on a sterile cot, he took a break from his steamed stare at the jail cell ceiling.

"Good. Good. One less revenge to go," Adam said.

Chapter Nine

Cain started to investigate what exactly happened to the Lincolns' neighbors. He remembered what Adam had long ago told him. "Son, if no one has ever called you crazy, then you haven't lived." Such was life for many in this West Kansas community. Such was life now. Farming families no longer were the masters of their own destiny. A dark curtain had long ago fallen to segregate them from the usual unusualness of the known fields, hills and natural gifts of the land, animal inhabitants and human interactions alike. A mystery was yet to be resolved. How did life change from a harmonious and regular calm into the harsh balm of outrageous misfortune?

Checks of the area newspaper records, looks at archives, and finds about what happened to local people revealed instances such as drug overdoses, mysterious illness hospitalizations and unexplained deaths. A psychiatric hospital, Wilson's Sanatorium, was mentioned in some of the newspaper reports. After a busy study of his medical books, Cain traveled to that location to look for answers, but the building, old and dilapidated, had been closed down. A place of shadows still required light no matter the means of the light's burial.

He pulled the Skylark into the driveway entrance and up along a dilapidated hole-spattered asphalt parking lot. Cain noticed a light shining inside the hospital building, so he decided to investigate further. He tried the doorknob handle, but it wouldn't immediately budge. A large picture window abutted the wooden door entrance, so he tried a look through the glass.

He found an old Security Guard sitting at the desk just inside the window area. He knocked on the window, which seemed to work as the Guard pushed back his chair, pressed a button under the desk edge and the front door clicked. Cain pushed on the door and it swung inwards. The Guard asked Cain's business.

"Just looking to find out a bit more about this facility for a family member." The Guard indicated he was scheduled for a Key round, but Cain was welcome to come along. The Key round commenced not without some explanation from the Guard. Each walk, called a "round", on the hour, every hour involved carrying a circular leather-bound clock about the size of a small cooking pot attached to a thin leather strap which the Guard held from his shoulder or swung along held by one hand. Inside the clock was a paper tape. When the Security Guard arrived at a metal box bolted to the wall, he opened by hand the lid of the box, pulled out the key which bore a number at the edge of the key, inserted it into an opening of the clock, turned the key until a punch mark was impressed into the paper tape to indicate that location of the building had been checked.

Cain talked to the Guard and learned much about the Witch rumors of Miss Pearl. The Guard said he looked at many of the old records which were left behind after the hospital was shut down, or simply stopped operating. Several inmates at the hospital were found starved to death, locked in their rooms, unable to escape. The Guard suffered a similar fate, as if a spell had been cast on the building and the surrounding grounds. Cain was shocked and wondered, "Did this fellow just say he was dead?" The Guard continued to speak matter of factly. Not able or free to leave given his work responsibilities, he knew some spirits of patients did leave and return. He learned some were residents of the town near where the Lincolns lived. They had gone to check on their loved ones, and also to attempt revenge against Miss Pearl, but they always returned to their place of death, as Miss Pearl, her Witch minions, the local Police Department, the Court system had not yet atoned for their many sins and it was not yet their time. Some of the hospital residents had atoned for their sins and disappeared from their place of death, but many others reserved time for one more sin to commit: revenge, as retribution for loss of family at the hands of Miss Pearl and her Witch coven.

"I am not sure how you were able to enter this building as a spell was rumored to have been cast upon it long ago. I believe that is why the patients and Guards all died."

Cain looked around. The words of the Guard burned into his mind like the solder from a fired-up soldering gun. He followed the Guard during his round of clicking the station keys into the Security clock. During the walk around, Cain could hear sounds, noises in some of the closed rooms. After the twelfth click, the round was done. The Security Guard finished at a desk near the front door. The desk was large. The top of it, adorned by wired bins of paper, revealed each had been marked by the handwriting of the Guard who kept records of each hour and day of his shift. Many of the entries simply read, "Round completed. No issues encountered." Three capital letters next to each entry, the Guard's name initials, verified the walk around had been completed. "A ghost's hand and record," Cain thought.

The empty parking lot outside, overgrown by patches of grass which had sprouted from the asphalt, bid a lonely picture through the large, rectangular window that served as a wall of glass next to the front door. Any Guard who worked a shift had been able to survey the parking lot from the desk. Cain now surveyed the landscape outside the window, from the Guard's perspective.

Cain searched for words. He shook his head a bit just to make sure he wasn't dreaming, that there was actually the spirit of a deceased Security Guard now seated at the desk, gazing out the window towards the parking lot. As he looked again at the Guard, he started to sense what happened. The Guard's body, face, flittered in and out as a complete human body, then parts appeared as exposed ligaments, muscle and sinew. The parts illustrated the emasculated remains of a boney corpse. It was in this stage of partial decomposition when the Security Guard looked directly at Cain. Cain noticed such while he looked out the window to his car. He feared to look directly at the Security Guard in this moment. Cain could see the Security Guard lift his hand of part flesh, part muscle, part bone and reach it out to touch Cain's side. Cain didn't move. He realized he had to determine if his mind, his eyes were playing tricks on him in this dim of hope place; this dower and dank world. He smelled death, but his mind had rejected the thought since he had entered the building. Cain realized he must ask a question.

"Those who remain here; do you think they would be willing to seek their revenge at a specific moment requested?"

The Guard didn't answer. Cain stopped his look at the Guard's window reflection, then turned and looked directly at him.

"Are some of those housed here, are they undead?"

The Guard's hand clenched into a fist and rested upon the desk edge, except for the boney thumb pointed up to the ceiling.

"Then it will be done," Cain stated. His voice echoed into the far parts of the main hallway. A cold wind delicately responded and caressed upon his face.

"I will come back, in the same car. It will be the sign to begin."

Cain slowly walked to the outside door, pushed it forward, and listened to the creak of the hinges as it rolled to a close. As he continued forward to the car, his thoughts of this experience surrounded him. He sat in the car, turned on the radio for some needed solace. Bon Jovi's "Blaze of Glory" floated in tune from the speakers. Cain looked over to the large windowpane next to Wilson's Sanatorium entrance. The Security Guard wasn't visible. All Cain could do was focus on thoughts of his father's face.

Chapter Ten

So, when the animal died, it must be eaten fresh, otherwise, it potentially became a Zombie and therefore competition in the newly dead flesh bazaar. Zombies didn't kill Zombies, in general, unlike humans and Witches.

The issue became, for the Lincolns, how to survive in a sea of filth; filth that was hell-bent on destroying the farm families and their remaining farms. Miss Pearl's Witch family bribed local authorities, friends of town families and others as a means to consume financially or otherwise kill off any resistance to her power schemes either by planned accidental circumstances or intentionally caused misery. Only a few free families remained.

Lilly visited Adam at the City Jail to help prepare him for his trial. The police had picked him up a few days earlier and charged him with the murders of the protestors in Meadow City. For the first time, her father confided the many issues unresolved in his mind. Adam remained plagued by visions of Eve during various moments of their relationship. It was a community of two that started out like a fairy tale. Each was young, still trying to find themselves in a world gone mad. Lines had unclearly been drawn between the Witch coven, non-aligned humans, and the town officials of Meadow City. No escape presented itself from a centuries long struggle. Allies and enemies crossed over and back among the three groups.

Adam's union with Eve started a trend of resistance, not so much because of one or the others reticence to yield, but rather, because together they displayed a need to seek their own way along the more difficult path. Each did their part in the yearly, monthly and even daily tasks of exercising the muscle of nonconformity. For the first several years of the marriage, they were clearly a team, openly displayed a thirst for their mutual commitment. After a while, as the road became rockier, less certain, each began to more readily question the true nature and impetus for the resistance in their hearts.

The wind aided their inability to keep hands clasped during the struggle, as if fate had made the decision for them. Eventually, Eve left Adam one innocuous day, and never came back. Adam went searching for her like a lamb in the barren field sniffed for a familiar odor. He found her, at Officer Clinton's house. Adam listened, from outside, to the sounds of lust and sexual interaction, as the pulled up interior windows allowed a douse in the bath of warm summer wind. He didn't enter. No need had presented itself. He burned inside of a hot passion coal, yet he wasn't able to stoke the fire any longer. Days later, the sound of Eve's voice and the blank, disinterested look in her eyes told him bluntly a love between them had died. A deep empty opened wide inside his spirit.

A light started to pierce Adam's vision. He started to awaken, but resisted the notion, relaxed and returned to his dream state in search of answers. His dream revealed on the day Adam and Eve died, Adam could see Eve walking in the barren field. He thought the lost lamb was returning. He went to greet her amidst a tornado warning, and each was violently swept away. The false god of "Change Is Good and Inevitable" had cruelly dropped the hammer. He realized change as an old coin; lost, found, re-used again. His life, her life had evolved into rebroadcasts along the same sound bandwidth.

His gut burned. Her eyes were blank. She mostly didn't look up at him. If she had, she would have seen two moist ponds about to overflow down a mountain ridge of his cheeks. His eyes were frequently, during this time, so wet and moist, when a tear began a stream down his face, he didn't bother to swipe it away any longer. He finally could not remain in the dream state, awoke, and allowed the sun from the near window burn into his eyes as he no longer wanted vision as a post death gift. He relented under the slight realization his sight may yet save him, and his remaining family and friends.

Lilly's voice finally broke through to his ears, "So that's how I think the City's case will go."

"Sure, hon. Sounds good," Adam razed as a response from his emotion cooked brain.

Chapter Eleven

The time for Adam's trial about the deaths he caused in Meadow City had come. Lilly drove him to the courthouse. Along the way she reviewed in her mind the legal defense plan she had devised and shared her thoughts with Adam. Her thinking, reasoning became infected by insidious thoughts: Zombies are people too, albeit DEAD people. Could she argue that the dead are people too? Still? Just people in a different form? No legal precedent presented itself, other than a plea of insanity or mental incapacity or self-defense. An angry mob had surrounded Adam in the town. Chaos reigned on the day in question. Adam looked at the individual members of the mob crowd. He could only think of them as a future meal. Their actions made such thoughts more realistic to him.

Lilly warned him, "Now is not the time for action. Now is the time for reflection."

Adam didn't look at her but responded, "Oh, I am reflecting all right."

Adam wanted to take the witness stand in his defense, as there were no witnesses in the prosecution's case to support him, even after Lilly's cross-examination. Prior to trial she had thought of trying to recruit some of the undead as witnesses. The thought of it was so outrageous, she rejected the notion. All that was left in strategy involved an impassioned plea by Adam, which he was happy to oblige. She prepared him for such a moment or tried to prepare him.

During his testimony which rang out more like the desparate man's speech, Adam said: "We are the meek, and we are here to collect our inheritance!"

The Judge clanked her wooden gavel hard into the sounding block. Adam continued, relentlessly.

"I am dead, yet you charge me with a crime of the living. I merely want to find my soul and leave this place, this plain, this town, this crucible of evil. "

Adam pointed to the Judge and Zelda, and others in the courtroom crowd, including Abel who had sold the tainted seeds.

"You Judge, and you Zelda, and you Abel, and all of you who have sold your soul to Miss Pearl. I merely wish to protect my family from your foul, greedy tentacles."

The Judge banged the gavel down like a blacksmith upon the anvil, yet Adam continued the steeled lash of his tongue.

"It is the time for the dead! The time for those who have been slaves to the greed and enmity of the wicked!" Zelda started shouting a chant, gradually joined in by those in the crowd, Witches, who helped carry forth her burning torch words of pain and havoc. Adam failed to relent, saying "Shout if you must. Scream chants. I am deaf to your attacks. I serve myself and family, my home, the ground upon which I have sown my spirit. I say your time has come. Mark my words, as the deeds to follow will burn into your bodies!"

Time for the Dead

The Judge's gavel broke at the handle. Zelda ended her chant. The crowd drew silent. Adam verbally ended on a last threat.

"When you see the purple rain, first in drops, then harder, faster, and when you hear them crashing down like bullets, then you will know, your time is done. Those you have betrayed will be avenged. It is time for the dead!"

Lilly looked over at Adam, who was still seated next to her at the defense table.

"Daddy, you seem lost in thought."

"Oh sorry. I was just imagining what I will say when it is my turn to speak."

"Daddy, you don't have to say anything."

Chapter Twelve

Eric Clapton's "Third Degree" played on Abel's headphones in the crowded Courtroom audience, audible to Adam. The sound calmed Adam, like the calm before a West Kansas storm. Adam sat in the criminal defendant's chair, next to Lilly. The Judge's appearance awaited to begin the legal proceedings. Lilly had graduated law school and recently passed the Bar Exam. In her first case she defended Adam. Adam's son, Cain, had gone on to medical school but had not yet finished as a second-year intern at the nearby largest County hospital.

"All rise in the matter of Meadow City vs. Adam Lincoln, deceased." The burley bailiff's rendition of the case name rang out like the sudden break of a violin string. The high courtroom ceiling obliged an echo in mocking gratitude.

The prosecutor, Miss Zelda Douglas, read out loud the charges of multiple murder counts. She waived her opening statement, as did Lilly.

Lilly had completed some background investigation on Miss Zelda before trial. Miss Zelda ran a powerful marijuana ring. Her land, adjacent to Lincoln's, extended over vast and deep acres of marijuana fields. As a Witch, Miss Zelda had been using her dark magic much the same way Adam and George used Zombie bites and meat feeding sessions to control the group they had secretly amassed. Zelda worked under the dominion of Miss Pearl who served as leader of the Witch coven. During a Pre-trial Hearing, Lilly had requested a Judge Trial so that no Jury would be involved as it would likely be controlled by the Witch coven anyway. The Judge granted Lilly's legal motion.

Adam determined to take the stand in his defense at the end of the prosecution case. As Lilly realized there was little hope of a successful defense after cross-examination of the County witnesses during the Prosecution's case, she aligned herself to Adam's plan. During his testimony, Adam provided the facts of his reincarnation in a rote manner, as he knew them, but his habit of wordiness in life also followed him in death. A little off base some of his words struck. Lilly requested a recess, of only an hour, but the Judge, in the back pocket of Miss Zelda's group, granted only thirty minutes.

A severe hailstorm had invaded the town and surrounding communities a few days before which knocked out electrical power and mobile phone communication due to cell tower damage. The power had just been restored, coincidentally, during the start of the court break. Lilly's mobile phone began transmitting previous messages.

Lilly checked her phone and in shock told Adam, while they were traveling to the first-floor lobby on the Courthouse elevator, she received a text message from Cain. It stated the only way to resolve the case, in his view: convert the Judge to the Zombie crowd, which may break the prosecutor Witch's spell power over the Judge. A bite near the brain stem might allow Adam to control the Judge. Adam could then exert his influence over the Judge, before Miss Zelda could cast another spell.

Cain had already rounded up some of the Zombies collected and housed by Adam in the barn and drove them to the courthouse basement in the early morning hours, just before dawn, where they remained until his signal.

On the way out of the courthouse revolving doors, Lilly and Adam could hear the beginnings of the Zombie feast which had delicately commenced. Adam suggested a stop into one of the local eateries around the corner. They stopped at a sandwich and pizza shop. Adam ordered his lustily imagined sandwich: two slices of rye bread painted by Ranch dressing, a thick slice of ham, a dollop of coleslaw seasoned by one tap of the saltshaker and two taps of the pepper. A cup of soup accompanied the order.

"Dad, you know you can't taste or smell the flavors." Lilly said.

"No, but I can imagine the aroma." Adam faux sniffed the delicacies, as presented to him by a jittery waitress when she clanked onto his table culinary instruments of bowl, plate, napkin, stubby yet wide tipped spoon. No knife. He and Lilly sat near the front picture window.

Adam advised, "Don't underestimate the power of soup." Lilly smiled. Adam devoured the sandwich upon its arrival like a wolf tearing apart a lamb. His lips challenged the soup spoon. There were no other customers at this time as they still served as meal product for the stealth Zombies feasting at the courthouse.

"Humans gotta' eat. Zombies gotta' maul."

Chapter Thirteen

When court resumed, Adam was back on the witness stand to complete his testimony. He intentionally badgered the Judge. Zelda began laughter at the prosecution table and evinced the gross gleam of an evil smirk. Adam had irked the Judge so much, she leaned over towards him, gavel menacingly grasped in hand. Adam then contemplated the first strike. The Judge's heartbeat banged loudly in his head. Her flesh aroma, the veins near popping out in her neck only served as balmy and visual culinary appetizers. The Judge continued to dip down her head from the higher realm of her chair, leaned her upper body towards him so her long black robe flattened against the bench railing as if upon a dining table, until Adam could no longer resist the entreaties of her magnificent succulence. He reached up and pulled down the Judge by the back of her head. The burley bailiff rushed like a football lineman, as he was so in size, but Adam zeroed in on the frantic vein, opened his jowls to expose cracked and jagged teeth, then noisily bit into the lower back portion of the Judge's plump head.

All hell broke loose in the courtroom as Zombies appeared from all door openings, at the Judge's Chamber to side doors for impaneled jurors, to the main entrance of the courtroom. The bailiff was smothered by Zombies and consumed adamantly as large portions of his meaty body sounded shred tears and pulled muscle pops inflicted by greedy clenched teeth. The female court clerk fled hysterically. A thin as a rail appearance perhaps spared her as a feast delicacy, or at least, won her the exercised discretion of a wasted effort by Zombie jowl claps.

The rushing Zombies overtook the proceedings in a crooked symphony of chomps and groans and satisfied throat sounds. The remaining courtroom crowd comprised mainly of Witches then rose and moved towards prosecutor Miss Zelda to close ranks of the Witch coven members. The now spell-chanting coven moved towards Adam and Lilly amidst the feast chaos.

PART THREE

Revelations

Chapter Fourteen

From the kitchen countertop radio, near the windowsill, poured the sound of Robert Johnson's "Last Fair Deal Gone Down". The sugar sweet notes rose upward to the ceiling tiles. Legend had it that Mr. Johnson sold his soul to the devil in exchange for musical talent. Some thought the devil made an unwise deal, as it was believed the ill intentions of the evil one would likely become melted by an elegant voice to which even angels could not resist the temptation of a good listen.

After the song ended, the radio station DJ blared a special report:

"Late yesterday afternoon, an incredible scene unfolded at Meadow City Courthouse when the accused murderer, Adam Lincoln, attacked the Judge and others in the courtroom during Lincoln's criminal trial. A month ago, many deaths were reported in town during a local college protest. The student protestors were peacefully chanting and singing in the middle of town. The subject of the protest involved use of artificially enhanced seed products by some of the farmers outside of town. Witnesses at the scene provided testimony in Court of unprovoked attacks by Mr. Lincoln. Some described his appearance saying he looked like he was high on drugs or drunk on alcohol. A college Professor and several students died as a result of the attacks ... ."

Since the Court day, Adam had holed himself up back at his farm. George sent to him several hundred Zombies for security. They were stationed in the barn to reinforce Adam's Zombie friends. Cain had installed a buzzer in the house, near the front door, in order to allow Adam to release the Zombies for an attack in the event the City sent any law enforcement to pick up Adam. Cain and Lilly had determined to stay at the farm in anticipation of the next cataclysm of disaster.

After a few days, all was quiet. Adam guesstimated the City duties of neutralizing him, his family and his farm had been passed on to the Witch coven and Miss Pearl. There was still the issue to figure on how to get a lock of hair from her as a means of entering the good graces of Miss Zelda. Given Miss Zelda hadn't sent out any minions to aggravate him about the mission, Adam figured he was granted a bit more time. Still, he thought it strange that a full out onslaught of misery, or at least a stern rebuke, had not been rained down upon him by his neighbor. He began to wonder, as was his nature, whether Miss Zelda had other, darker plans for Meadow City and the surrounding Counties. He wondered who was really running the show; Miss Pearl or Miss Zelda?

Lilly and Cain realized eventually they had to tell Adam about what really happened on the death tornado day. Eve wasn't there at the house. She had already left after a long, adulterous relationship with one of the police officers by the name of Clinton. Adam acted stunned.

"My memory voice says George told me and you told me, but I still couldn't believe it."

Lilly further related that Eve worked with Clinton and the police to help take over the farmlands targeted by Miss Pearl and Zelda. This more bad news pierced Adam's mind. Every word and syllable of each word stung him like a wasp in his mind and in his heart.

"You didn't die in a tornado," Lilly advised. "Officer Clinton shot you in the back, while you were staring up at the stars on a clear night," Cain added. Adam then verbally rationalized some meaning.

"I think I remember. I was trying to figure out how to get us out of the financial mess your mom had put us in. The money mess was so great, the adultery indiscretions were buried by it, I guess."

Lilly and Cain looked at each other for some agreement whether Adam understood.

"I guess sometimes, love bites," Adam stated matter-of-factly. He tried not to let them see how much his insides burned like red hot coals at such recalled revelations buried deep inside him.

Cain and Lilly alternatively explained to Adam some of the episodes of events after his death. Eve had become cattle for Miss Pearl. She was sent to the homes of farmers, to seduce them; then Miss Pearl's minions blackmailed the seduced paramours into paying for silence about the transgression. Those who ran out of blackmail money ended up losing the farm, the land, house, and their family. Some of the blackmailed committed suicide; some fought back futilely as vengeance; some disappeared in disgrace; but the confiscation of land continued, unabated by counter effort or zeal.

Miss Pearl would launch attacks against the vengeful using the police as her surrogates. Some of the stubborn who had yet to succumb were rounded up by Miss Pearl's Witch coven, taken to her house, and were never seen or heard from again.

A few more evenings passed. On one forlorn evening, marked by more dying crop lands, mysterious missing cows, and the tortuous thought bombs of a lonely soul, Adam determined he should walk the long distance to the neighboring farm owned by George Pullman. Adam had not heard from his friend in a while, so he wondered how things were going for George. The silence of impending extinction spurred this thought onward.

Night had descended upon the land again; too many nights of no action. The cool breeze that enveloped the Lincoln's front porch spurred an energy in Adam.

"I guess it is time," he thought.

He stopped the rocking of the chair with a push of both feet upon the porch floor. He looked up towards the western sky and noticed Jupiter was in the Ascendant. Sagittarius was Rising.

"Yes, it is a most defin ... defin ... itely ... time."

A blackness in his mind suddenly began to disperse like clouds, in the manner as when they reveal a poke from the Sun. Cain came outside upon the porch to check on Adam.

"George might know what it means. He knows a lot about the stars," Adam noted.

Cain knew something was up when he no longer heard the creaking of Adam's rocking chair runners against the porch wood.

"I'll run you over to George's in a few days. Working on some medical studies right now."

"Okay, son, okay," Adam said.

"Finally," Cain muttered to himself, "Time to clean this backed up cesspool of the chaos gone amuck."

Chapter Fifteen

A few days later, the dust had rustled in the driveway of George's property again. Adam lurched in measured steps up the front porch steps, as Cain backed the Skylark out of the driveway and left. Adam looked around at the cavernous void, then shouted, "George!"

"Be there in a sec. Some personal maintenance in progress," George bellowed from inside his house.

Adam knew to make himself comfortable as he sat himself into one of the rockers strategically placed for visitors. George creaked open the porch door. The retraction of it against the frame signaled his arrival, then he took his customary rocker meeting seat.

"So, you ate the Judge?" George confirmed.

"Sure. No other way out."

"Makes sense, given the circumstances," George agreed.

"The world's infected by idjits and assholes," Adam moaned.

George could detect Adam's irritated state. "Can't all be that way, or we wouldn't know normal," George stated.

"Okay, except us and our kin," Adam said, more at calm as he sighed a bit to release some irritation from his mind.

"Right. I'm sane and you're crazy," George posited. They laughed a good laugh together.

"Bingo," Adam said.

Together, they continued another porch meeting and a long talk. The meeting purpose, in Adam's mind, was to plan a means to stop Miss Pearl and her Witch minions. George's mind was on something else, which he soon revealed.

"I found this bit of knowledge, courtesy of the god Google," George laughed. He reached his hand into a shirt pocket, pulled out a wrinkled folded paper, opened it and read aloud.

"Jupiter is the light when all others go out. ... If Jupiter rules your chart (as your ascendant) or your Sun, you were born under the lucky star. Jupiter's sign is Sagittarius, the sign of optimism, faith, and prospering from risks others wouldn't dare take. Jupiter's transit to a planet shows the forces of growth in play."

Adam spied the western sky. Jupiter smiled down at him. Sagittarius stood ready at the bow.

"We have 'til the end of summer to make things right, or our time is lost," George counseled.

George suggested they use the bad seed he had stored and not yet used, by mixing the seed with raw meat and giving it to the undead who resided at his place and at Adam's place. George stood and descended the porch steps. The moonlight gave them a path of light. Adam followed. George walked up to an old barn, pulled the latch, then entered.

"I thought this thing was put out to pasture," Adam wondered.

George called out, "Come on man. See what we have here."

Adam followed to just inside the doorway. Slits of moonlight beamed rays from parts of the roof and the high parts of the sides. Only the moonlight revealed George's hand poking along the wall for an object still mysterious. George dug into one of his shirt pockets of which there were many, plucked out a wood stick match, scratched it along a leather belt hung against the wall, then attempted to light a hurricane lamp resting on a mantle next to the leather belt. Adam stared hard into the dark of the interior. He couldn't make out any sight of objects or creatures.

"What's the smell? You're composting in here?"

"In a manner of speaking," George offered.

Having accomplished a broken smatter of light from the lantern wick, George pulled on the lantern by the handle and slowly moved it around to a darkness spot in front of him. So, they tried an experiment.

"Our Adiemus," George remarked.

Adam looked a bit puzzled but went along with the idea.

"We try this and see where it goes, if it works, I mean," George explained, "our Adiemus moment."

The Zombie horde, stooped low in the dark at the opposite end of the barn's interior, began to betray the silence in scattered foot slides and low-sounded groans. George offered a meat piece mixed with the bad seed to one undead and then waited to see if it created a more sentient presence in the undead eater.

The experiment succeeded as evidenced by head bobs and tiny twists at the neck and a somewhat enlightened gaze on the face of the test subject. The two tried it again on another undead. It worked again. They tested words like "Stay, sit, roll over" and each command worked after some practice. The undead tainted meat eaters became aware enough to take orders and respond positively to George and Adam. In this way they were able to transform the legion of the undead into a command able physical force, and perhaps, an army against the Witch hordes. Just outside the barn, George and Adam reconvened.

"Our dogs of war," Adam stated.

George rubbed his chin; looked up again at Jupiter's direction in the heavens and offered one more piece of advice.

"You know I am pretty good at predicting, feeling, the changes in the wind."

Adam concurred. "Everyone in the County knows that, George."

George then spoke in a mystic's voice. "There are robust winds, bad winds, the kind that cause mayhem; crash, crush, destroy all in their path and around it. They are coming, like a legion of Angels from the heavens. I don't know why. I just feel it, deep inside me."

Adam thought and thought about this enlightened counsel. He knew from experience and their long, family friendship, such counsel was not offered lightly or carelessly. These words from George had been carefully woven, like the material of a seamstress, into tight, regular threads; created a picture as reliably enchanting as the painted Italian portraits and scenes from antiquity.

"I get your drift, George."

They went back over to the comfort of the front porch, sat together in silence, to give the seed time to do magic and to give them more time to plan. They rocked and rocked back and forth in the chairs, chewed on George's previously verbalized thoughts, the star visions, and the fate the gods had presented to them.

"We have to get ready, George."

"Yes. Make ready. This time is our last and only chance to make the difference."

George's certainty comforted Adam more than any other moment of time since his unexpected rebirth.

"You look tired," George said. "Why don't you just nap here for a bit?"

"Sounds good, thanks," Adam said.

George entered his house for some relief from all the cogitating.

This brief interlude is brought to you by Culture TV, care of Adam's dream state. Some of the living humans fought back after it was determined their efforts to save their own lives would not be chastised or punished when defending themselves against the masticatory proclivities of the Zombie protected class. The government didn't grant this exemption out of simple integrity or fairness. It was allowed to help control a steadily increased Zombie population proliferation.

Government agencies began to study Zombies who owed back taxes. Do humans who regenerate into Zombies still owe taxes when they come back to life as undead?

Cloning issues faded into Zombies multiply fast and reappeared in immigration of Zombies' problems. The dream weaved towards a sophomoric nature infusing many of the day's leaders in politics and other institutions such as universities, think tanks, media prognosticators and culture merchants.

More weaving of the sewing needle changed the vision into the arena of harassment laws, views of tolerance or intolerance. His mind had never latched onto an understanding even in the wake of life. View discrimination entered the workplace. To not look at or associate towards a Zombie became an insult, despite how dangerous the relationship experience, as the Zombie could eat a human at any time. Thus, people had to work with them, literally vomited, some involuntarily while around or near

Zombie co-workers, but in order to avoid harassment in the workplace laws, employers were required to hire a certain number of the undead. The no-smoking laws were a bit odd. It wasn't lethal to some around a dead person, yet the laws extended to that situation also.

Zombie advocates argued, since undead were not of the living, it was discriminatory to apply the laws of the living, however, the laws were so vague, when it fit the Zombie purpose, advocates could claim protections under the living laws. Living laws and undead laws competed in the legal swim pool. Crapping in the pool was allowed.

Zombies who had been outed resorted to wearing makeup to hide their appearance. The issue whether appearance hiding was legal ensued. The lawyers cleaned up financially on this issue and many others.

Some Goth types wore Zombie makeup to become woke. By the way, zombies eat living flesh, to stay alive, what would the law say about that? The dream skidded on two wheels into another thought escapade. Zombie protestors appeared in colleges, universities and some cities to advocate in favor of Zombie rights.

In the calculated, lawyerly chaos, Zombies accrued more rights than living people, as living people could only claim living rights, yet Zombies could claim the rights of the living and the rights of the undead. Advocates of suicide started to sprout like a plague among the culture, grounded in the argument it was better to accumulate rights of each status, living and undead. A brief mass movement of suicide ensued so the living could take advantage of the living undead legal exceptions.

The management head Zombie of a secret government biochemical nanotechnology reanimation project buried deep inside a spy agency had planned all of these proceedings to take advantage of the laws for the undead. The government organization plotted to take over the land of the living according to the headline and subsequent outed story of a national newspaper.

Eventually, a Zombie for President movement started up. The Zombie candidate won the election, then convinced the Federal congress that people were better off dead if they were not tolerant of Zombies. Some other countries had already adopted such a civil system.

Eventually it was discovered in some scientific studies the mere existence of a Zombie created noxious chemicals, like cows, so global warming anarchists convinced the population that Zombies were bad for the environment, therefore, they must go. Funeral homes cleaned up profit-wise on double and triple burial ceremonies.

Could Zombies reclaim the wealth they had lost when they died?

Adam awoke. "Geesh, almost don't want to sleep anymore. That stuff was exhausting."

Chapter Sixteen

Lilly determined to dig a little further into the Witch world. She identified a possible helpful source to mine: Miss Pearl's lawyer. The lawyer usually frequented a local Meadow City drinking establishment when released from his legion of work chores on Miss Pearl's behalf. A planned accidental meeting might become a good research opportunity.

Seated at the near vacant bar, intentionally next to the disheveled lawyer, she offered to buy him a drink. He obliged. A few soft words; some visual exchanges; then she struck the gold to open his mind. Miss Pearl's lawyer became enamored of Lilly, perhaps as an ear to capture his reckless voice, so she bought him drinks until he became pliable enough to reveal Miss Pearl's operation, and his role in it. He was a rather handsy bastard. As they sat ensconced in the dusty shadows of a booth in the dead-end portion of the establishment, the lawyer revealed he had arranged to abscond with a good portion of Miss Pearl's ill-gotten money.

Lilly asked the lawyer, "How do you plan to escape?"

He answered he was still working on it. The lawyer then passed out with a loud head bang onto the wooden table surface and caused utensils and plates to bounce the bounce of the musical jar.

"Better than nothing," Lilly said out loud. "Better than nothing."

Chapter Seventeen

After the Judge in Adam's murder trial was converted to the Zombie side, Cain had confiscated her body and dumped it at Adam's property, then staked it to a metal chain to await any possible reincarnation. After his meeting with George, Adam tested some of the bad seed on the Judge. She eventually arose in an undead state, although not nearly as sentient as Adam's state, a mystery still. Adam determined to use the Judge's new mastication skills as a possible defense to make a visit to Miss Pearl's mansion.

They together walked the way from Adam's farm to Miss Pearl's property. The trip gave Adam a good look at the property, the layout. He was surprised no sentinels had been stationed to run interference. Perhaps Miss Pearl didn't consider him a threat. "Good," he thought, "do please underestimate me; horribly underestimate me," then he strayed like a too curious dog into boasting territory, "till death do us part." Wheat fields in the distance, as far as his eyes could see, reflected an audible hum in the wind fingers and against stronger invisible long lines of waves. The evidence of fertile thriving seed was everywhere spread in Miss Pearl's plains.

When she found out it was Adam, who at the mansion door introduced the Judge only as an associate to gain entry to the premises, Miss Pearl agreed to meet them, at least through the words of the front door emissary, likely a Witch or pawn thereof; Adam wasn't sure. During the introduction to Miss Pearl, Adam strained to see her face as it was covered in a thick black veil dotted by stars and demon-like eye stitches all around. She was seated, comfortably on a large couch, the back of it against a wall painted in many designs and symbols and beings not of this earth. Miss Pearl seemed to be taken aback when she viewed the Judge. Adam didn't quite understand why.

He tried to remember George's counsel of "Keep an open mind to the fields of possible; thereafter, weed accordingly." Adam spoke to himself, "I can't believe I remembered that."

"Remembered what?" Miss Pearl asked. Her monotone voice masked her emotions.

Adam searched for an answer. He sensed "Nothing" would not suffice as a response.

"My wife's face," he said after digging deep down to mine out a response. It was his true thought.

"Oh, yes. So sorry for your loss," Miss Pearl said.

"Believe me, I will try hard for you to become as sorry about it as possible," Adam imagined saying. He wasn't sure if Miss Pearl could read his mind or not. He almost didn't care.

"The weather hear is so unpredictable," Miss Pearl said.

"Yes, almost predictably unpredictable," Adam thought.

Silence took hold as each of them sized the other up, down and sideways. Adam took solace in remembrance of music from The

Cranberries, "Zombie", for a time anyway. A boiling hot pot of circumstance wafted an aroma to him, at least a smell he recalled as his sniffer no longer worked so well. He wished he could taste a cranberry. Death had taken from him many senses. He refused to wallow in the loss. Undeath provided many regrets, but it had not yet lasted so long as to need a memory bookshelf to store them. Something else mattered more. Cain and Lilly; his friendship with George; a newfound course of the gift of undead life; how to specifically make it matter still eluded the grasp of his withered flesh hands. He needed to relearn how to play the human game. He remained a novice in the world of Witches. He knew he was an easy enough kill in their world; and if not a kill, an animal to become caged in their spell world. Many of his human memories remained whispers in the undead sentient brain imprisoned in a cage of bone and sinew his skull had become. "Many discoveries to be unearthed yet", he thought. He mentally brushed off the dirt like an archaeologist.

Patience, despite the crush of time; understanding, in spite of the moments needed for revelations to evolve, dogged him endlessly. The search for a rose absent thorn continued. In life, torn skin and thoughts dismayed him; in death, they became irrelevant; in undeath, he was granted a unique opportunity to observe the blight, yet not suffer physically as a result. Just needed to find the right doors to knock on. Just. Just. Must. Must. Why? Why? No answers yet. No answers. Wait. Wait. His mind could hear the wind. That was a good start. Reminded him of his point on the planet, the country, the county, the farm, a patch of dirt. He realized he led a life somewhat devoid of climbing, for he feared the fall. Such fear no longer existed in him. His undead vision seemed clearer than his live vision.

Lilly had filled Adam's mind of her Miss Pearl's lawyer meeting story, and the subsequent rumors of his disappearance. Miss Pearl's lawyer had informed Lilly, at their saloon meeting, of his plan to involve the State level authorities to expose Miss Pearl's schemes. The lawyer thought he was immune to her power because of a mythical necklace which provided defense against Witch's spells. He had obtained the necklace from another Witch who he didn't know worked for Miss Pearl. The necklace wasn't hexed. It was a hoax; a paid for set up; one of the many Miss Pearl plotted against the populace and those who crossed her. The lawyer was imprisoned in a narrow dark room just below Miss Pearl's main room, through a trap door, where she intended for him to die.

The lawyer started screaming for help, very muffled screams, but Adam could hear them. "Must be the lawyer Lilly told me about," Adam thought. He didn't let on that he could hear the lawyer, but his facial expression didn't deceive Miss Pearl.

"Pardon me. This house has many voices when the wind has its way."

"Oh, I quite understand," Adam lied.

"So, who is your friend, the one who accompanied you?"

"Another suffering the undead disease," Adam answered.

Everything out in the open. The only question became whether Miss Pearl would kill now and splatter Adam and the Judge into tiny pieces in one swift, curt spell incantation; or whether two blood hungry Zombies could rid the West Kansas plains of the scourge, a master Mage Witch empowered by generations of knowledge and experience. Judging by past and present actions of her minions, Miss Pearl harbored a temperament to utilize this advantage to exploit the entire region for her own purposes, as long as the benefits of such power filtered down to the existing Witch coven support. Else, why a need for minions? And a growing number at that? George could figure out the scheme, Adam considered.

It was time for Adam to leave, but first, the plan must commence, for better or worse.

Adam spoke, "I don't have many friends left."

Miss Pearl stood, walked the few steps separating the airy wall of the room between them. Even this close, Adam could still not penetrate the dark veil enough to read her eyes.

"You want me to protect your children," Miss Pearl stated directly.

Adam posed, "Yes. A doctor. A lawyer. Useful to you, perhaps."

"How dare you to assume what is and isn't useful to me," Miss Pearl stated abruptly.

"Not a dare at all."

"Silence!"

The distraction worked. The Judge, too close to the potential human kill, banged into the back of Adam and knocked him over as the blood and chew rage took over. An attempted chomp took a lock of blonde hair that rested serene and unguarded just below the lower edge of the hanging black veil. Miss Pearl shouted words not intelligible to Adam's ears and the Judge began to crumble in the lower legs. The spell words consumed the Judge into a plague of gray dust upon the floor. Except for the lock of blonde hair which parachuted down next to the pile. Miss Pearl's eyes so flooded the room, she apparently didn't notice a part of her hair had been clipped off by one single bite. Miss Pearl called a minion for assistance in a loud and matronly tone. Adam attempted to collect himself, stood after much effort and creaking of bones and stretching of ligaments and muscle. He tried to ask, "And about my children?" but Miss Pearl had vanished; how and where Adam was uncertain.

Just before the aide minion's footsteps transformed into physical entry of the room's doorway, Adam snatched the blonde hair shards and grasped them like a lifeline in one hand. Upon the minion's entry, no sparring words or heeds of woe were exchanged. Adam simply walked out of the room and let himself out the front door. The walk back to the farm was refreshing. The wind tickled him as much as the senses of an undead man could be tickled. The Sun's rays slowly bore down to the level of the horizon to mark an end of day in the West Kansas plain. Along the way, Adam wondered if the imprisoned lawyer had become an undead. Also, he couldn't help but wonder why Miss Pearl's voice sounded so familiar to him.

Chapter Eighteen

Cain sat at the Lincoln's kitchen table and read a medical book in preparation for another case at his medical internship. The kitchen counter radio provided instructions on how to know the signs of a tornado.

"Weather forecasting science is not perfect, and some tornadoes do occur without a tornado warning. There is no substitute for staying alert to the sky. Besides an obviously visible tornado, here are some things to look and listen for:
1. Strong, persistent rotation in the cloud base.
2. Whirling dust or debris on the ground under a cloud base -- tornadoes sometimes have no funnel!
3. Hail or heavy rain followed by either dead calm or a fast, intense wind shift. Many tornadoes are wrapped in heavy precipitation and can't be seen.
4. Day or night - Loud, continuous roar or rumble, which doesn't fade in a few seconds like thunder.
5. Night - Small, bright, blue-green to white flashes at ground level near a thunderstorm (as opposed to silvery lightning up in the clouds). Extraordinarily strong wind is snapping these mean power lines, maybe a tornado.
6. Night - Persistent lowering from the cloud base, illuminated or silhouetted by lightning -- especially if it is on the ground or there is a blue-green-white power flash underneath."

A loudspeaker beamed the sound of ABBA's song "Dancing Queen", rumored to be Miss Pearl's favorite song to the extent she had it piped into every room of her mansion. The sound of the music found a way into the large field outside the mansion. The Zombies recruited by George and Adam gathered onto the and along a natural hill boundary between Ms. Pearl's land and Adam's land. Those gathered from the Sanatorium visited by Cain couldn't resist the sound and began a dance among the undead. They danced across the field onto the top of a small ridge, lined up next to each other in rows. Some of the Zombies at the top of the hill carried kitchen brooms. They tossed upward the brooms.

"I taught them how to do that," George said, then beamed a smile.

"Impressive, as is your outfit today. You smell good. When did you become a Monk?" Adam asked.

"Just a few adjustments. Bathed in Saint John's Wort to relieve fear. The necklace is to convert any spells; the attached little charm bag holds cloves and other spices. Brought a few more tricks of the Witch trade I will show you at the right time."

A wind began to blow over the hill and into the fields. As if an over-excited puppy, a small tornado formed from the columns of dark, low clouds in the vicinity of the boundary of Adam's dead fields and Miss Zelda's live fields. The clouds continued to sweep across the landscape in obedience to the wind gods, accompanied then by another infant tornado, and another, and another, and another, until there were five descended side by side from the now almost coal-black clouds hung down like a curtain of iron. George had obtained earplugs and cotton balls for another and larger horde of Zombies from the surrounding towns, and they couldn't hear the music.

Adam's charge rang out loud and deep, "Time to bring on the heartache!"

The jury was still out on whether love or hate would win the day; or whether a combination of the two could reach a truce as a hung jury. No sweet caress; no light touch; no rub upon the hair in smooth, longed for strokes. No more index finger pointed traces along lean shoulders. None of that needed. The habit was broken, ripped, torn with all the rage of a drug addicts withdrawal tremors. All that kind of touching bridled in betrayal was about to die a cruel death; and yet, still not cruel enough, for Adam. Patches of silence in the wind stew shook him away from the emotional strangle hold of vengeful thoughts. A thirst of no resolute satisfaction could he find in this moment, but he would use the stimulation for the good of his family now.

He had no more faith in love. It only existed for him, in his mind, as a beast to be broken, tamed, like a wild horse. He let it back into the field, to find another pasture, as it had worn out the welcome. No more words; no more thoughts, although they had haunted and plagued in life and death and after death. A spell it was, he sometimes rationalized; the only reason he could grasp and not vomit out in disgust. He had missed her, Eve, so much; one more allowed squeeze would have busted her heart outside of the chest cavity; and he would bite it and devour it and digest it and crap it back out. The crap would fertilize the wheat fields and the cycle could then start again; go on forever. No. That option skipped town long ago. George looked at Adam; began to wonder about Adam's sanity.

"Get your head back. Caustic thoughts will not devour Miss Pearl."

"No. No they won't. You're right. Working on it. Working on it. Working on it." Adam couldn't get his head right.

Some of the Witches came marching out, parade-like, then opened wide and outward along a healthy swath of the grassy area. Towards the Zombie horde they moved, seemed to float, all lined up, one Witch for every ten Zombies. A pageant of death elegantly progressed. George sprayed some red powder in front of himself, then turned to Adam and sprayed a line in front of him.

The long and colorful peasant dresses of each Witch flowed like the ripple of a slow stream over rock impediments at the sandy base. Each of their calculated steps lightly touched, moved the blades of grass all around, and a wind helped accentuate the parade, pressed against the grass and moved it outward like ocean waves. The Zombies stood in their death clothing of now torn threads and popped buttons; disheveled and broken in appearance, adorned by the fleshy flays of errantly rotted skin patches. The genie oozed upward and outward of the bottle. There were no wishes about to come true, Adam thought. George seemed strangely more optimistic.

"At least they aren't attacking us yet," George said.

"Don't worry. It's coming. Then we will unleash hell," Adam chided as he imagined fury in a side-glance to George.

Within about ten yards of Adam and George, the Witches stopped their forward movement. The zombies stood crooked, lined up like a long dilapidated Chinese wall; staid, solid, unmoved; stared at the Witches; stared through the witches; zoned out or zoned in, it looked the same. Adam felt a weakness inside his stomach; the weakness that always pulled him back from a sense of impending disaster. He had no reason to pull back the emotion bomb inside him. "Let me unleash the rage," he pleaded with himself. "What the hell. I'm already dead," he rationalized.

The Witches wore faces like portraits. Unmoved, solid, frozen masks their faces showed. Adam and George looked at each other, then looked out upon the scene.

"What the hell?" Adam asked.

"I think something is about to happen," George said.

"What, what is about to happen? We should charge them now."

"Or not happen. Yes. Not happen. Incredible." George rubbed his chin, pulled his left ear, cupped his right hand behind his right ear.

"Hear that?"

"Honestly, still not used to the idea of being dead yet still walking around, but yes, hear that. What in the heck is it?"

Silence started to fill the void as the wind retracted, escaped, hid; got out of the way; buried itself into the nothingness in which it could retreat; like a magician, disappeared its touch; waited cautiously, or patiently. Difficult it was, to interpret this wind; for what purpose unknown; perhaps the next pounce of forever touches upon the skin, tree, leaf, window shudder, clothesline sheet, wheat reed.

"The weather has suddenly become our ally." George noted.

"What da' ya' know," Adam intoned softly.

He pulled on his lower lip too hard and a patch stripped off and fell, straight down, landed softly into the grass at his feet. As he noticed his feet, gray in color, he waggled his toes.

"Hey buddies. Good to see you."

He then turned and waved at his Zombie allies.

"What?" George asked.

"Nothing."

"Nothing's good." George agreed.

Adam turned back towards the Witch lines, then looked down to focus his ear holes. He could hear the clouds behind rattle and jostle like Hussars about to lower their spears and charge full bore into the Witch crowd.

George stated, "Okay, the time for philosophizing is over."

"Right." Adam agreed. "Time to bring the wowch."

"The what?"

"The wowch. That's a hurtin' that screams a wow and ouch."

"That hurts to hear," George said. He could tell Adam was nervous. Not a good sign for a Zombie mind.

"See, working already," Adam taunted back.

The wind song continued to change tone.

"Hey, I rotted under the ground for a long time. Plenty of time to think," Adam offered for George to further chew upon.

The Witches had become the wheat, the grain, ready for cutting down, pulverizing, making into food stuffs for another day. Then a voice, like a banshee shout, arose from one Witch in front and center of the group.

"We are not here on Miss Pearl's accord. We are here of our own." Her booming voice shredded away some of Adam's skin in tiny pieces. His Zombie allies suffered in the same manner.

Miss Pearl's mansion, about 200 yards away and a bit up the hill, behind the Witch line, shuddered. The size of it expanded, widened, arose from the ground as if alive, until it was the size of a medieval castle.

Adam couldn't resist a dig. "Ain't that quaint."

"When there's nothing but a dream, fear can hide," George piped up. "It could be a mirage, casted upon our vision to trick us into retreat."

Adam grimaced. "Don't get all Irene Cara on me, Sir. Now is the time."

"Your passion is showing, bigtime." George remarked calmly.

Adam had another idea that popped like a cruelly swollen zit from the center of his nose. "I have an idea."

George couldn't resist. "Is it doable?"

"Miss Cara it is, then. I am going to ride this feeling to the end, of Miss Pearl, the Witches, or myself. No disrespect to you, George." Adam felt he was on a role now as he tried to psyche himself up for the inevitable, either glory or defeat, nobly born.

"None taken. Do you want to hear the idea?" George asked calmly.

The Witch banshee spoke again. "We can see the passion in your eyes. We know what you want, and why." The voice crashed into their brains.

Silence reigned again like frozen ocean waves. George had become desensitized to looking at the Zombie faces in his barn. He sensed no passion in them; only an everlasting thirst for flesh.

"She's just trying to confuse us, George," Adam stated, "Isn't she?"

"We're not backing down," George sternly stated to the Witch.

Then George whispered to Adam, "Summer ends tomorrow. It is now or an autumn of discontent, forever."

"Right. We can't hold back now. We lost everything around here. The losing stops now," Adam talked sternly, towards the Witch.

"Enough!" The Witch banshee's voice boomed so loud both Adam and George had to cover their ears, rocketing their hands upward towards the tiny caverns on each side of their heads. The lack of sentient nature in the Zombie horde didn't reveal a similar effect, although a hunger urge was becoming a stubborn problem in need of a solution, and immediately. The banshee-voiced Witch then tossed some small white pellets into the air. The other rows of Witches responded in kind until many pellets filled the air in a near white blanket above their heads.

"What's that?" Adam asked George.

"Rice, to bring rain."

"Time to get it on, Miss Witch," Adam remarked. Then a pitter, then a patter; another pit; another pat; then a splat.

"Something just hit me on the head," Adam complained. A faint thunder sound started up the beginnings of a heavenly symphony. Adam reached up his hand and patted the top of his head as the hand searched for a clue.

Miss Witch observed, eyes closed, "It is raining."

"No, it isn't. Get out of my head, Witch!" Adam bellowed.

A rain of methodically increased intensity started. The grass opened wide to provide a cup for containment of the Witch conjured wetness.

George looked behind and up at the clouds on the ridge, just 100 yards behind them. The row of Zombies on the hill started a slide towards an unknown target. The Zombies below the hill, on the ridge just behind Adam and George, meandered, mouths open like newborn chicks, and absorbed each quarter-sized rain drop as if chocolate mints were falling. Some of the drops had transformed into hail stones, popped out holes in the Zombie faces; knocked out some eyes; tore off an ear or two. The surreal scene only gathered momentum.

Miss Witch remarked, "The grass; it is gray. Storm. A big one," as the drops began to pelt onto the crusty, hard Zombie bodies.

The clouds hovered at the ridge, in hues of gray, black, and gray black, and darker black. "About as disturbed as I've ever seen them," George said.

"Don't look now but some of your friends are leaving," said the vocal acolyte Miss Witch.

"Oh geez. Some of the cows, the few that are left, must have got out of the fenced area," Adam whined. A thunder rolled in the clouds, echoed throughout the valley two and three times.

"Adam, no. She is conjuring a spell," George said. He reached his closed hand out to Adam and dropped an acorn into Adam's overalls side pocket. "Helps to protect you from a storm."

Sound of moving water and lots of it started to sting their ears.

"The Witches conjured a flood from the run-off stream that rims the edges of the western fields for miles," George advised.

"Dang. They can do that?" Adam asked.

The flood bore down upon the plain like a locomotive, crushing and rolling over every living and dead and undead thing. Some of the Zombies that descended into the lower area of the plain, out of hunger, were pile driven through and away in the violent quaint scene of chaos. All would be over soon, or so thinking of the visibly over-confident Witches betrayed.

Adam and George, who had moved up the side of the hill to escape the conflagration, looked at each other knowingly. They exchanged a glance of "We've got them now."

"Maybe that was the secret Lilly learned from Miss Pearl's lawyer?" Adam wondered out loud, "but she never told me what it was."

George asked Adam, "What's worse than walking zombies, or running zombies?"

"I don't know. I give up. Hints welcome," Adam said.

"Flying zombies," George said.

"How you going to do that? Are you a Witch?"

"Warlock."

"A Warlock? You've been holding out on me," Adam said.

"No. I mean a male Witch is a Warlock. I'm not one. Look, don't hold this against me, but my wife, Edith, was a Witch," George finally told Adam.

Adam thought for a bit, at least for the bit allotted in the time of this field battle. George continued. "So, anyway, I learned a few things, you know?"

"All ears," Adam said.

"A rebound spell," George said.

"A rebound spell," Adam said.

"You'll see, if I can get it to work."

"But you're not a Warlock."

"Don't have to be. Just need a force able to rebound the spell; a physical force; and I think it is coming this way, from behind us."

Adam asked, "Can I start my rant now?"

"Go for it," George stated, in his best imitation of a stern Rocky Balboa voice.

"Nice."

Separated by the temporary river of water, Adam started on a conscience release rant that increased in the same degree as the flowing water level receded. Almost poetic it was, in the tone. Up and down surfing waves, zooming high, cresting soft. He began to address random thoughts that raced through his cranium of a carefree highway, even in tense moments; because of tense moments.

"Love? Love? Love doesn't deserve another chance. No. No more chances with love. Goodbye. Get lost. Lock it in a closet. Smash it with a baseball bat. Bury it. Peace!"

Miss Witch looked at George, not so much concerned as confused. A rolling thunder sounded in the distance. There was no point in talking over it. The symphony needed to play out before the applause.

George felt obliged to explain to Miss Witch, and to Adam. "Sometimes he has trouble turning down the noise of the pain." Now more eyes were looking at George as the zombies seemed intrigued by what words may artfully dab at the canvas of their predicament. George then created the words he knew would do justice to Adam's predicament.

"Trauma is no stranger to Adam Lincoln. Poisoned by Miss Pearl's seed; cheated upon by his wife while she was in cahoots with Officer Clinton; Adam cornered by the anxiety of a cheating wife, then entrapped in a wooden box and underground for a year; only to find the last sense of being he could hold onto, his land and his children, became a target of an abominable scheme cooked up by a near immortal Witch. At least his children forged onward, survived and thrived. Go figure."

Adam could hear every word of this diatribe. "I think even the Zombies could hear you, George."

"Masked in my words, Adam, I included Edith's spell incantation for a rebound hex. Been practicing it for a long while. Some of the Zombies I practiced on didn't survive it, except in many pieces after."

"Maybe you have some Warlock blood in you," Adam conjectured.

"Maybe, so," George stated in a prideful tone, "erugif og."

Adam looked around, up, into the eyes of Miss Witch and George, yet he couldn't find a single word or phrase to release the tension inside him. He remembered, when Lilly was still little, as a child, she read the Bible. He checked a bookmark she had left in place at Psalm 91. He saw the words in his mind and said them aloud. "He who dwells in the shelter of the Most High will rest in the shadow of the Almighty." Adam realized he had been in that shadow, in his coffin, only a few months ago. He was fueled now; a locomotive of energy. The words George uttered had stoked the engine like coal shoveled into the furnace.

"Erugif og," Adam repeated, over and over.

"One more thing, Adam. Take this knife and stab at the wind as it approaches. The wind will know what to do."

"You sure, George?" Adam asked. "Seems a bit odd."

"Sure, as day," George said.

A low guttural sound began to emerge into the atmosphere. It mirrored a wind in the clouds; then the clouds began to spin like tops; then they moved over and down the ridge. It was on. The jailbreak of jailbreaks. The Zombies were pushed forward by the invisible hands of the swirling and violent winds. The Witch parade pushed their arms against their side and hands onto their thighs in a crouch so as not to reveal the tender learnings of the lower body, and to chant a now unintelligible mantra.

Adam couldn't let go, or rather, his mind couldn't. "Your kiss is tainted now. Nothing can be done. No apology. No penance. Done! Just, done!"

George mercifully interceded. "Adam, duck!" George hit the ground prostrate and Adam turned around, pushed by the wind onto his back. The mud helped them stick to the ground. Four mini tornados had crested the hill behind them; sent hundreds of Zombies into the air like missiles which proceeded to randomly strike into the right flank of the Witch horde. An extreme mess of blood bolts and body parts rolled and twisted and exploded into the muddied field below.

Miss Witch attempted to quell the wind ferocity, but to no avail. The more she tried, the stronger the winds blew and the closer they came: the rebound. The force of the wind almost clogged out gruesome sounds of bone breaks and ripped body parts. The waterlogged and mudded ground rolled up and transformed into long patches like new house carpet rolls readied to be installed. As it further unfurled, bodies living and undead were covered, almost completely along a large swath of the field plain. Two of the tornados, as they began to recede, hit the side of the remaining central Witch troops and knocked them down like bowling pins.

Some of the Witches flew up and down in the wind currents, some to rest hard into the ground like lawn darts, some twisted into balls of flesh and blood twine as they rolled along the ground like tumbleweeds smashing into each other or flown away by the hands of the wind. The only untouched Witch, in the end, stood tall in the messy field's middle, as if immune to the elements of the earthly world.

George and Adam started to run as best they could towards the less muddy and more solid portions of the plain dried by the tornado winds, to make their escape from the conflagration and play their parts in the mansion assault. George observed in huffy breaths.

"That one in the middle may be the leader; the strongest of the bunch. The wind swirled in a circle around her but couldn't knock her down."

The assault upon the house ensued in earnest. All seemed over until one, soft and silent tornado remained, chugged slowly towards the point of attack: Miss Pearl's mansion, looming halfway up the next hillside. The renegade tornado hovered, darted, meandered as if lost, found, uncertain, certain, then made a direct line for the house. Adam and George were astounded.

"Looks like that one has a driver," Adam remarked.

"You're just seeing things. Wishful thinking," George said, although his face remained inquisitive.

Adam looked closer. He sniffed the wind, for what it was worth.

"George, there's something, or someone, in that last tornado."

George squinted as best he could under the conditions.

"I think you are right. Poor soul."

"Wait a minute," Adam shouted.

"Why?"

"I think I know who that is, in the tornado," Adam said.

Time for the Dead

"No," George's voice expressed in doubt.

"Yes!" Adam's voice beamed a light of hope.

The tornado was driven by Eve.

"Dang, that woman has a mean thirst for vengeance in her," Adam said, in near cheer intensity. Adam looked and looked. A tear began to slide down his grayed face.

"I never saw you cry before. It's happening again, isn't it," George said. "That song, 'Love Story' by Andy Williams is playing in your head."

"Where do I begin … ," Adam damply responded as emotion had extracted another drip from his eye. " … even now she fills my heart … Wait. Wait a sec. I just remembered a smell; Officer Clinton's smell, on Eve's clothes. Time for sentimental gibberish to exit my brain." Adam banged his right-hand, balled into a fist, against the side of his head. "Ready."

George's plan involved convincing the Witch forces to think the Zombie troops of Adam and George, thin in numbers as demonstrated by the field troops, would then cause the Witch forces to let down their guard and allow Cain to guide the greater number of Zombies around to an old cave entrance that went underground and behind Miss Pearl's mansion for a sneak attack. The plan worked like magic. A frontal assault by an Eve driven tornado helped to spur on the cause.

Adam and George slogged along to the mansion in the soaked

plain, marked by many body parts of the Zombie remains and Witch bodies in gray and brown repose, some no longer a party to the sentient world. Eve had wreaked havoc with a vengeance.

Adam asked George, "Where do you think Witches go after the Grim Reaper makes an appointment?"

"To be determined, my friend, to be determined."

"I hope Cain is okay," Adam expressed in a concerned mumble.

At the mansion, they came to realize, there was no Miss Pearl and no living thing left, except some animated body parts of comingled, wind-twisted Zombies and Witches. George theorized the Miss Pearl legend, created by Miss Zelda as an alter ego substitute minion Witch designed to stand in at matters of ceremony, redirected the blame for the devious plot to take over the City and surrounding Counties. Apparently, the lock of hair mission for which Adam was promised a reward, served as Miss Zelda's plan of an Adam suicide endeavor. He had survived and all the events leading up to this "now" moment started a fall into retribution place.

Adam and George, after reviewing the misery of the mansion assault, moved over to the large front room window to study the carnage. Miss Zelda stood on the field, looked around, and glowed in the Sun to bask in her final victory and the insidious nature of her dominion control.

George loudly asked, "How did she get … ?" Adam screamed, "Get me over there, somehow, now, please!"

George looked around the main room. Nothing. He moved to the hall and opened doors to other rooms. Nothing. He opened another door near the end of a hallway. The room identified a janitorial closet. An old, somewhat curve handled broom leaned against the wall next to shelves of what appeared to be sanitation supplies, but a closer look revealed potions bottles, organs and human and animal limbs in fish tanks apparently filled with preserving or embalming fluids. "Darn. Everything including a broom." The broom responded, floated over to George.

"Well, what do you know," George said as he reached out to grab it by the handle, had second thoughts, found a cloth, and used it like a glove to grab the broom. He walked back to the supposed Miss Pearl's room.

"Look what I found," George showed Adam.

"No way," Adam shouted, as body parts wriggled among them.

"Way," George answered, "but I don't know how it works."

Just as he finished the words, the broom started to pull him towards the main hallway.

"I have another idea," George said.

Adam followed the thought, "I like where this broom is going, I think."

"Right. Miss Zelda must have summoned it to help her escape

the muddy field," George said.

"Ready," Adam said. He mounted the broom. "The winner takes it all, George. One last reckless act, for the win."

George advised, "Stay low. Just one moment in time."

"Say goodbye to my kids, and I love them."

The broom and Adam attached, body pressed against and along the handle length sped out on a last mission ride like a torpedo. The broom soared straight up the arched cathedral ceiling of the main Hall as an opening emerged at the top on cue to allow the broom exit. Adam rode as passenger. George ran across the bloodied floor to a window at the front of the mansion.

The broom swooped high over the field and descended towards Miss Zelda. George could see her reach up for it. Energy beamed from her every pore as she released it in a cleansing of joy and glory to celebrate herself in honor of her victory. The broom stopped directly in front of her. The stopped motion of the broom allowed Adam's body velocity to strike, headfirst, mouth wide open to make a bull's-eye strike at the Witch's throat. George couldn't hear it, but his mind imagined the clamp sound upon the cervical vertebra; the tear sound of the outer flesh; the pop and rip sounds of the shredded ligaments. The strike was so clean, so precise that Miss Zelda's head propelled upward into the air, directly from the point of her body cavity at the neck. The head spun around like a pitcher's curve ball, then dropped downward and landed, then stuck into a groove the skull weight pressed into the mud.

George strained a look at the spot where Adam's body slid along the mud and slush and pockmarked field detritus. The signs of a body plant stretched out like a water slide along the ground. George ran to the front door, pushed it open, jumped down the steps and partly ran towards the scene of their transgressor's demise, but he couldn't see Adam.

George squinted. Rubbed his eyes. Shook his head side to side and looked again. There he was. The Zombie of all Zombie's; the breaker of the spell; the Witch assassin himself: Adam Lincoln. The front of his body lay blanketed in a layer of mud head to toe. His head and eyes pointed to the sky; arms spread wide.

George thought about Adam, "He can't wait for those stars to come out tonight, and neither can I."

Chapter Nineteen

Necrophilia, the urge to socially comingle among dead things, became the newest and most fashionable fad. Adam had become a cause celeb nationwide. Interaction among dead things exited the realm of psychological illness; paraded in a grand entrance of social thought, if not otherwise slowly seeped into social discussions like a leaky faucet. Best friends were dead, but not so much. If the bad seed lay buried among the lifeless body, the dead could resurrect after a year or so.

Funeral music transformed from the somber, morose sounds of Chopin's Funeral March. A more jovial tone took hold of those deemed popular, as Irish and Scottish dirges abounded. The end of one life, briefly mourned, became celebrated by the potential for rebirth. Amidst the aftermath of a chaos gone mad, Adam Lincoln was elected Mayor of the town. Was there any doubt? It was primarily a town of Zombies. The Witches had gone into hiding, at least, those who remained. They were still around; came to town sometimes, but not much conversation ensued.

In the meantime, Adam could boast that maybe, one day, he would become Governor. With any luck, maybe even U.S. President. He went around saying Lilly and Cain were working on it, anyway. That was good enough for those still absorbed by the human realm. For the Zombies, not so much interest. Only available food met the test for maintenance of interest. The cattle crop began to revive and grow, such that the Zombies remained happy enough. The wind paid no mind. Like a thief in the night, it came, the wind, to strip all things; objects and the sprites of the seeds that grew from the soil; and the animals that trod the ground; and the sentient beings that molded all into a viable existence alike. None were left to plead for the mercies of subtlest discrimination; and the wind glided; and the wind roared; and the wind stripped all clean to satisfy a greedy lust no sense could fathom. For the wind, devoid of reason, ambled along the riverbank of purpose, and the purpose poured on and out and through; to be discovered by humans, animals and objects affected by the mysterious path; over and over, in waves; in tidal storm mode, until all was readied to start anew, on a fresh, clean landscape.

No real, tangible answers. Adam posed the question, "What is life?" He thought about it as he rocked back and forth on the porch while seated in a rocking chair next to George.

"What do ya think, George?" George rocked along in a rocker as old as the fields. He pondered a long time, yet no answer was immediately forthcoming. More contemplation was necessary, allowed, as time was on their side now.

"George."

"What, Adam?"

"Do you hear that sound?" Adam listened intently, enamored by the sound he had become so familiar with that he could almost not hear it.

"What sound, Adam?" George listened. "Sort of like a clicking?" George pointed towards the setting sun.

"Well I'll be," Adam intoned. "George. You're an old devil. You lassoed the Sun."

"I did," George said. "Wait for that cloud to cover it."

"No offense, you know, George."

"I'm not old, do you think?" George laughed.

A medium sized cloud drifted over to and covered the Sun. Adam could then see something dangling, rocking from the tree limb, attached to a rope holding the object.

"George. Why is Eve hanging like a Christmas ball from that tree branch?"

"To remind you about what is important," George said.

"Important. Yes, you are correct, Sir," Adam agreed. "I have to remember that; what is important."

"Eve's jaw clicks sound like sweet music now," George said.

"Maybe she's happy," Adam replied. "Reminds me of that Bob Seger song, 'Against the Wind', don't you think, George?" Adam asked. George nodded in the positive.

"To remember, Adam, is most certainly a precious gift," George reminded.

"Sure is, George. Sure is."

Time for the Dead

George asked, "How are the kids doing?"

"Cain returned to medical school to complete his internship. By the way, he found and helped Miss Zelda's lawyer to get off a drug fix. Lilly is at the law library in town, working on a new legal case."

The answers and perhaps too many questions merely blew in the wind, audible to those who knew how and when to listen. As a sound bounded off of object and ear flesh, then became trial and error intelligible in the communication, a purpose cycle was yet to be determined; but Adam and George had set their mind on a purpose, so it was just a matter of time before one great wheat field of curiosity sprouted in the plain to turn the page. The Harvest Moon smiled.

"Hey George. Got any good stories?"

-

--

If you enjoyed this book, don't forget to leave a review on Amazon!

I highly appreciate your reviews, and it only takes a minute to do.

Also, by Mike Gutowski: CRATCH

www.ingramcontent.com/pod-product-compliance
Lightning Source LLC
Chambersburg PA
CBHW071529100726
47908CB00004B/1333